D1388231

This book should be returned to any branch of the
Lancashire County Library on or before the date

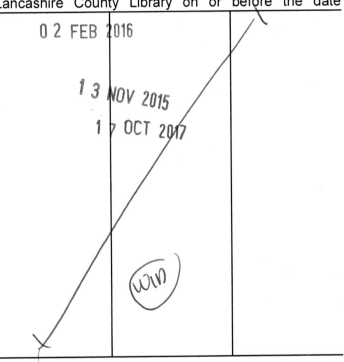

0 2 FEB 2016

1 3 NOV 2015

1 7 OCT 2017

WID

Lancashire County Library
Bowran Street
Preston PR1 2UX
www.lancashire.gov.uk/libraries

*Lancashire*
County Council

NeWest
PRESS

# THE KILLER TRAIL

D.B.CAREW

# THE
# KILLER
# TRAIL

## D.B. CAREW

NeWest
PRESS

Library and Archives Canada Cataloguing in Publication

Carew, Derrick, 1969-
        The Killer Trail / Derrick Carew

Issued in print and electronic formats.
 ISBN 978-1-927063-52-1 (pbk.).--ISBN 978-1-927063-53-8 (epub).-- ISBN 978-1-927063-57-6 (mobi)

        1. Title.

PS8605.A737K55 2014          C813'.6          C2013-906955-0
                                               C2013-906956-9


Editor For the Board: Don Kerr
Cover & Interior Design: Greg Vickers
Author Photo: Tanya Carew

NeWest Press acknowledges the financial support of the Alberta Multimedia Development Fund and the Edmonton Arts Council for our publishing program. We further acknowledge the financial support of the Government of Canada through the Canada Book Fund (CBF) for our publishing activities. We acknowledge the support of the Canada Council for the Arts which last year invested $24.3 million in writing and publishing throughout Canada.

201, 8540-109 Street
Edmonton, Alberta | T6G 1E6
780.432.9427
www.newestpress.com

No bison were harmed in the making of this book.

We are committed to protecting the environment and to the responsible use of natural resources. This book was printed on 100% post-consumer recycled paper.

1 2 3 4 5 15 14 | Printed and bound in Canada

FOR
TANYA

# ONE

*Tuesday, February 7, 4:13 p.m.*

He approached James Carrier's body, not so much to ensure he was dead—the gaping hole in the chest pretty much confirmed that—but because Ray Owens always liked to inspect his handiwork. He had done his job, and he had done it well. He'd studied his target—knew where he lived and worked, what church he attended, even where he bought his cigarettes. Most importantly, he knew James Carrier walked this trail every Tuesday. Ray had waited patiently for the right time, the right shot. Now he congratulated himself on a job well done.

The only blemish on this otherwise perfect job, he thought, was the *fucking* crows. They cawed in annoying unison, as if to give away his cover. For a moment, he considered using his Remington M24 to shred a few feathers. *Nothing ever stops me from enjoying my kill,* he scowled. But he lowered his rifle, not wanting to waste bullets on a few pathetic birds. Besides, he knew he wouldn't stop at one; he'd kill them all.

Ray emerged from his cover in the bushes, slapping snow

from his clothes as though swatting away flies. He deftly disassembled the rifle, stowing it away in its case, where it would remain in preparation for the next job. He reached into his tattered trenchcoat and pulled out his cell phone to call his client.

"It's done." No response; he didn't expect one. He dropped the phone into his pocket and grabbed a cigarette. He didn't know much about his client, and this suited him just fine. All he needed to know was who, when, where, and how he was getting paid.

Nor did he care about the *why* when it came to his targets. He remembered his foster mother always asking those stupid *why* questions: Why, at age ten, had he severed her cherished lovebird's head? Why, at twelve, had he punctured his foster sister's eye with a pellet gun? Why, at fifteen, had he set his principal's car ablaze? His answer was always "Why not?"

Ray didn't waste his time trying to understand his actions. All he knew was that a kill gave him a rush unlike anything else he had ever experienced. Even sex was no match for the euphoria that came from inflicting pain and sorrow on others. He left the whys for others to worry about: the school counselor who had told Ray's foster mother that he had difficulty forming attachments and didn't interact well with others; the child psychologist who had diagnosed Ray with conduct disorder; the head shrink at the Institute of Forensic Psychiatry who had diagnosed him three years ago with antisocial personality disorder. None of it meant squat to Ray. The only thing that mattered was that he'd been able to carve out a nice little niche for himself: *Have gun, will kill.*

Leaning down, cigarette dangling from his thin lips, he brushed his greasy, thinning hair away from his forehead and drawled, "Are those crows bugging the shit out of you too, J.C.?"

Ray grabbed his rifle—his constant companion—and began his retreat from the trail. During the hours he'd spent waiting for his target, snow had accumulated around his scraggy body. Now, a sudden snow squall ripped through the woods, ravaging branches like so much dead wood. He wasn't sure where his next job would take him, and for now, he really didn't care. He just wanted to leave this godforsaken place for a warmer, drier spot, where he would wait for his next call.

# TWO

On a scale of one to ten, Chris Ryder figured this run would rate a dismal three. He had long ago taken to rating his runs: ones were horrid and tens life-altering. He lived to run, but on this cold and blustery day, it hurt to breathe, and each step he took trapped him under inches of unforgiving snow. Today's run would certainly reach no higher than a three.

*Well, Ryder, you've got yourself into a fine mess now.* He knew that it was stubborn routine that had taken him to this trail. It was Tuesday, and Tuesdays were running days. So run he would, come hell or high water—or, in this case, a wintry hell.

Woodland Park, outside Vancouver in the Lower Mainland of British Columbia, was an area Chris usually loved for its natural beauty. On most days, he also loved the thrill of the unexpected. He'd seen deer, coyote, and the occasional black bear. On most days, the terrain's steep inclines and winding switchbacks provided a decent challenge for his athletic thirty-eight-year-old body. On most days, he cherished the adrenaline rush and the clarity of thought that came from running on these trails. This was not one of those days.

This was one of those days Chris wished he'd charged his iPod. The sounds of shrieking guitars and pounding drums would have been a welcome distraction.

It occurred to him that running and music remained the only constants in a life that had become foreign to him. The past six months had been memorable, despite his desperate efforts to forget. *"Chris, I think it would be best if Ann Marie and I moved out for a while."* The words of his wife, Deanna, played over and over in his head, no matter how hard he tried to erase them. He had trouble grasping this new reality where he was reduced to being a visitor on Tuesdays and Saturdays with the two most important people in his life.

He wondered how things had gotten to this point and if he'd ever again experience the wholeness and contentment he was searching for. Since the separation, he'd had offers for dating, but he just wasn't ready to try love again.

He felt alone here on this desolate trail where the only other living creatures were the crows incessantly screeching in the distance. *Damn, I'm pathetic*, he thought even as he welcomed the companionship they provided.

Chris tried to shake the depressing thoughts from his mind and focused on his struggle with the snow-covered trails. He knew that time, like the weather, was working against him and estimated he had twenty minutes before the last traces of daylight surrendered to the night.

He hadn't wanted to be running this late in the day. He had planned to skip out of work earlier, but had been delayed. Paul Butler, a despondent patient at the Institute of Forensic

Psychiatry where Chris was a social worker, had pleaded with him to talk just a little longer. Chris had found himself spending an inordinate amount of time at work lately. Helping others with their problems seemed a lot easier for him these days than resolving his own.

He tried to remove thoughts of work from his head, to focus on getting through his run and keeping to his schedule. Chris and Deanna had worked out a plan where their daughter would stay with him on Tuesday and Saturday evenings. This meant he had less than two hours to get to the house he had once called home to pick up Ann Marie.

Reaching the crossroads area of the park, a familiar point in his run where three trails intersected, he noticed another set of footprints. He wondered whether a foolhardy routine had driven another victim like him to this frigid trail.

His eyes caught an object jutting out from the snow. Curious, he reached down to pick it up: a cell phone case. Yanking off his snow-encrusted gloves, he opened it to find a cell phone inside. Chris reckoned it had been dropped only minutes before, judging by the snow accumulating on the trail. With no one in sight, he flipped the cover open and scrolled through a variety of features on the phone, hoping to find a number that would put him in contact with the owner.

No luck. Chris tried the redial button, congratulating himself on figuring out a way to reunite the lost phone with its owner.

After three rings, a commanding voice answered. "Yes, Ray?" The man sounded mildly annoyed.

"This isn't Ray. I have his phone."

A brief silence was followed by a perplexed "Who are you?"

"Chris. I was running the trails in Woodland Park and found this cell phone. I wanted to let the owner know I found it, but there weren't any numbers except yours."

More silence. Then: "All right. Ray will want it back. Wait where you are, and I'll have him meet you."

Chris sensed this guy was used to barking orders for others to follow, and he didn't feel like playing along. "Listen, I've got to be somewhere. It's almost dark and the weather is turning out here. I'll leave the phone at the gas station on Cumberland Street, across from the entrance to the park." A tree branch smashed to the ground with a thud, distracting him.

"Chris, I understand the inconvenience this creates for you, but I'll have Ray there in a matter of minutes."

Chris picked up a sense of urgency in the man's voice. "Listen, here's what I'll do. I'm heading back—" The phone lost reception. Chris shook it, and the signal returned. "Are you still there? I'm heading back to my truck at the park entrance. I'll be there in about fifteen minutes. If Ray is there, I'll give him the phone. Otherwise, I'll leave it at the gas station."

"Thank you, Chris. Now, how will Ray recognize you? I assume you are alone?"

"Yeah. I'm alone. You won't find too many other fools out here tonight. And I'm wearing a yellow jacket. I'll be the one freezing his ass off."

"Thank you for your cooperation. We'll see you in a short while and take care of this." The line went dead.

Chris' thoughts suddenly shifted to his daughter, and he groaned. Her mother would be sure to give him grief for messing up her night. Realizing he'd left his own cell phone at work, he decided to use Ray's to call Deanna. Ann Marie answered.

"Hey, sweetie, how are you doing? It's a lovely night out there, isn't it?" He surveyed the broken branches littering the trail around him.

"Where are you, Daddy? Mommy's been calling you."

"I got caught out on my run. Can I talk to Mommy, please? I love you—"

Before he could finish his sentence, a flustered Deanna was on the phone. "Chris, where are you? I've been trying to reach you for the last hour."

"Sorry, Dee, I decided to go for a run at Woodland before picking up Ann."

"You're joking, right? It's a blizzard out there. Are you crazy?"

"I wish I were. Joking, that is." He wiped snow from his head. "No, I'm out here and I found a cell phone. Someone's coming to pick it up, so I'm going to be a few minutes late coming over to get Ann."

"That's what I was calling about. I think it's best Ann Marie stay here for the night. It's getting too stormy for her to go out tonight. Is that okay with you?"

Chris knew she wasn't really waiting for an answer, that she'd already decided what was best for the both of them. He also knew she was right, but he would try to salvage something from the night.

"Would it be okay if I came over to see Ann after I finish with this phone business?" While he knew there was no longer any hope of reconciliation in their marriage—they'd been down that road to nowhere in the past—he hadn't given up on trying to reach common ground with Deanna, if for no other reason than the health and well-being of their daughter. The product of a broken marriage himself, he was determined not to make the same mistakes as his father.

"You're welcome to drop by. Ann Marie would love to see you. And Chris... Be careful. This sounds pretty dangerous, meeting someone you don't know, in the middle of the woods, in the middle of a storm."

"Well, Dee, what can I say? I'm a sucker for punishment. I guess I should go. It's his phone I'm using, and the battery looks like it's about to die. I'll see you soon."

Silence at the other end. The call had gone about as well as he'd expected. Deanna's tone told him that she was not happy. He wondered if the change in weather had resulted in a broken date for her. Chris shook the thought from his head and resumed his exit from the trail.

# THREE

*Tuesday, February 7, 4:53 p.m.*

C.L. slammed the phone onto its base and glared out the window of his three-million-dollar estate, trying to suppress his rage at Ray Owens. The one time he'd asked him to do a job, and the bastard had messed it up. Now Ray's stupidity threatened to expose him. C.L. had heard the stories about Ray and knew he was a loose cannon, but he'd needed someone who would carry out the job of eliminating James Carrier without asking why. More important, he'd also needed someone who could not be connected back to him. Ray had fit that bill on both counts. Now that bloody phone was joining them at the hip.

This would be the last job Ray would do for him—the last job he would do for anyone. And C.L. was going to have to clean up the mess Ray had made. He lumbered his potbellied body into his home office where he unlocked his filing cabinet. His eyes scanned his private Rolodex until he found the card he was looking for. Punching the numbers with his fingers, he stared at the windblown snow outside the window, relieved to be snug inside.

His call was answered on its first ring. He wasted no time in idle chitchat. "You in town? Good. I need you to take care of something for me. I've had a job go sideways on me today. I want you to put it back on track." He disclosed the details of the assignment. Pouring a glass of Glenfiddich, he slammed the bottle down on his oak desk. "I know it's snowing!" he roared. "I don't care what it takes or what it costs. I need this done tonight. Can you handle it?"

Receiving the answer he wanted, C.L. picked up his glass and took a generous sip. "It's at Woodland Park, near the gas station on Cumberland. The guy's wearing a yellow jacket. The name's Chris. Do him, and Ray. Yes, Ray Owens. And bring me that bloody cell phone."

He hung up, a grin spreading over his face. *Money talks*, he thought with a smile, and took another swig.

# FOUR

*Tuesday, February 7, 4:57 p.m.*

Ray carelessly drove his truck with one hand on the steering wheel, the other frantically searching his pockets for his cell phone. "Fuck!" he shouted when he realized he must have dropped it at the park. He knew he was in a race against time to retrieve his phone before anyone else found it. He thundered his rusted Cherokee down the snow-filled road, his eyes scouring the area for the nearest pay phone. Spotting one a half-block ahead, he careened his truck into the inside lane, bringing it to a screeching halt before jumping into the phone booth. He dialed his cell phone number. "Don't answer," he snarled. As much as he hated the idea, he'd rather retrace his steps all through the dark, snow-covered trails than hear a voice answer on the other end of the line.

"Hello?"

"Who is this?" Ray growled.

"Chris. You must be Ray."

"How do you know my name?"

"Your friend told me, and he said he'd have you come by to pick up your cell. How soon can you get here?"

Ray's thoughts ran wild. Who was this asshole? Why did his voice sound so familiar? "Uh, who did you call?"

"I don't know the name. I couldn't find any names on your phone, so I pressed redial and I talked to the guy who answered."

In an instant, it was clear to Ray that his boss had been contacted. His bony fingers squeezed the phone as he pictured wringing Chris' neck. He knew exactly what C.L.'s next move would be. He would have to get to Chris first, collect the phone, and use it as protection against C.L. But who the hell was Chris? "What did you say your name was?"

"Chris Ryder."

Suddenly, it came to him. Ryder was the social worker at the shithole IFP. Ray had served twenty-two months in jail after a psychiatric assessment at the Institute suggested he was fit to stand trial on charges of aggravated assault. But he had even bigger reasons to hate Chris Ryder. *I'm gonna like fucking you over, Ryder, just like you fucked me over.*

"Where exactly are you, Ryder?"

"I'm on my way back to my truck at Cumberland. Your voice sounds familiar. Do we know each other?"

"We'll soon find out," Ray replied with an alligator smile.

"Yeah, just hurry. I'm not—" The phone's battery died.

# FIVE

*Tuesday, February 7, 5:04 p.m.*

Chris shook wet snow off his jacket. He smiled to himself, thinking Deanna would probably want to smack him upside his head if she were there. She'd say Ann Marie had more sense at five years of age than he did being out here now, and he knew she'd be right. *You're always right, Dee. Even when you're wrong, you're right.* His fingers were aching from the cold, his soaked running shoes making his toes numb. It was getting dark now, and not expecting to be on the trails at this hour, Chris was without a flashlight. Leaning forward, he kept his eyes on the ground to avoid tripping as he made his way slowly back to his truck.

He stopped suddenly, as his eyes detected something in the distance—something lying conspicuously on the ground. A chill ran up his spine, but this chill had nothing to do with the cold. Heart pounding, he inched his way towards the shape, trying to focus on the shape against the onslaught of snow on his face. Then a feeling in the pit of his stomach threatened to turn his insides out. He no longer felt cold; he no longer felt wet; he didn't know exactly what he felt, but he knew he had never felt like this before—because he'd never discovered a body before.

Chris stared transfixed at the blood-stained body. The shock led to a bout of vomiting. He struggled to keep his head from spinning as thoughts rammed into each other. In an instant, he knew several things. The man had died a violent and unnatural death, judging by the pool of maroon blood that had leaked from a gaping chest wound and spilled onto the white snow around him. A wave of sorrow swept over him when he realized he'd seen this man before. Their paths had crossed many times on these trails, and they'd always greeted each other in passing. Why would anyone kill him? Who would do such a thing?

As the gravity of his grisly discovery began to settle in his mind, Chris realized his own life could be in danger. He instinctively dropped to his knees for cover, looking wildly all around to see if anyone was there. He crouched against the base of a huge red cedar and struggled to compose his thoughts. He replayed the steps he'd taken during his run. No, he hadn't met anyone on the trail. His mind fixated on the cell phone he'd found and the peculiar conversations he'd had with two people who sounded desperate to have it back. *Holy shit, I may have talked with the killer and told him my name.* Streams of sweat converged with a heartbeat so thunderous Chris thought his chest would explode. He focused on slowing his breathing and organizing his thoughts. Who had he been talking with? It was some guy named Ray, who sounded strangely familiar. Where had he heard that voice before? *Oh my God, what have I got myself into?* Chris finally connected

**THE KILLER TRAIL D.B. CAREW**

the voice with the name. *Ray—Ray Owens.*

There was no doubt in his mind that Ray had been involved in this killing. It had been three years, but Chris would never forget him. In his ten years at a forensic psychiatric hospital, Chris had worked with men and women who had done unimaginable things to other human beings. In most cases, a deteriorated mental state had influenced their actions. He could see beyond the terrible acts to the tormented minds that ultimately responded to treatment and rehabilitation. He'd helped these individuals take progressive steps toward restoring their mental health and reforming their lives.

Ray Owens had been the most notable of exceptions. When Chris had worked with Ray, he didn't see torment. He saw a psychopath, a man who reveled in his ability to inflict torment on others. Ray was admitted to IFP for a psychiatric assessment due to the sheer brutality of his crime and his astonishing insistence that his actions were justified. He'd defaulted on four months of rent. His landlord, a frail, elderly man named William Dobbin, called upon Ray one night after neighbouring tenants complained of noise coming from his apartment. Ray responded by seizing Dobbin's cane and bashing in the old man's head with it. Dobbin subsequently suffered a fatal heart attack while recovering in hospital.

Dr. Stevenson, the treating psychiatrist at IFP, found no evidence of an acute mental disorder with Ray. She concluded that he was in full control of his faculties and actions, and in court he was found fit to stand trial. The upgraded charge of manslaughter was not approved, and Ray spent less than two years in jail on the lesser charge of aggravated assault.

Beyond the brutal, senseless act that had robbed an innocent man of his life, Chris was disturbed by the way Ray had portrayed himself as a victim. Ray seemed appalled that he'd been charged, and even more outraged at being ordered to undergo a psychiatric evaluation. Chris remembered Ray's disparaging remarks about his co-patients: "They're goofs, and you're an even bigger one for thinking you can help them." Ray had made the lives of his co-patients a living hell, to such an extent that Dr. Stevenson fast-tracked her assessment of him to discharge him from the hospital and send him back to court.

Chris also remembered Ray for another reason—a reason that made him feel ashamed of himself, a reason that made him question his professional principles and personal values. He had come to hate Ray Owens. Ray had an uncanny ability to get under his skin. Despite his attempts at burying his contempt towards him, he knew it lay just below the surface. Chris had been relieved to see Ray removed from hospital and out of his life. Now he shuddered at the thought that the man was back.

Chris realized he could not return to his truck. The park entrance would almost certainly be a death trap. His only recourse now would be surviving the night on the trails. This prospect terrified him in a way that he'd never before experienced: he knew what Ray was capable of doing to him, and just as disturbing, he knew what he wanted to do to Ray.

His thoughts returned to the cell phone. He tried to squeeze one last bit of juice from the phone's battery to seek help, but it was useless. In frustration, he was about to hurl the phone against a tree but stopped himself as he made the connection between the cell phone and the body he'd discovered. He had what the killer wanted—and would kill to get back.

Chris' mind raced as he struggled to compose himself and

make sense of his crisis. Thrust into the middle of a deadly plot, he couldn't resist feeling sorry for himself. *Why me?* Up until this moment, he'd spent most of his time either agonizing over his broken marriage or struggling with career burnout. He could never have imagined his life getting any worse. And yet, it *was* worse. His very life was in danger. That knocked him from self-pity to survival mode—fight or flight. Right now, he knew he had to run for safety.

In an effort to clear his mind, Chris shook his head. He knew these trails and could use them to his advantage, starting by veering off the main path into deeper brush, then finding a hiding place where he would wait out the night. And he knew the perfect place—an old, abandoned shack he'd discovered several months earlier. The cabin had been used as makeshift lodging in the years before hunting wildlife had been outlawed in the area. *Hey, Ray, don't you know hunting is illegal in this park?* Chris could almost picture Ray's twisted reaction, which was why he was now the hunted. Even worse, his footprints would be visible to the trained eye, so he just had to gamble—and pray—that the dark would work in his favour and that he would lose anyone following him by taking a meandering course to the cabin.

Chris was shivering uncontrollably. His running jacket was not waterproof, and the combination of body sweat and snow had rendered it almost useless against the cold as it clung damply against his body. *You'll catch yourself a death of a cold, Ryder.* His legs ached, and as he walked the sound of cracking branches under his feet reverberated like gunshots. His rumbling stomach reminded him he hadn't eaten in several hours, and the last of his reserves had been wasted when he'd puked them out. But images of the dead body he'd seen quickly put all creature comforts out of his mind. If he didn't stay one step ahead of his pursuers, this would be his last night on earth. He'd find cover for the night and make a run for safety at first light. *I will survive this.*

# SIX

*Tuesday, February 7, 5:24 p.m.*

Ray had guessed right. He'd figured C.L. would dispatch a hitman to take him out, so he waited patiently at the park entrance for *his* prey to arrive. He recognized Dale Goode, a man known for specializing in the disposal of bodies. *You may be Goode but you're not good enough,* Ray snickered. Ray had him in his sights the minute Goode stepped outside his oversized white Chevy van. He let him take a few steps away from the van before he fired a bullet into Goode's forehead. Ray watched in morbid fascination as fragments of bone, brain, and blood erupted into the air, scattering into the black night before settling onto the white snow. *Another one bites the dust!*

Ray dragged Goode's body along the ground to the rear of the van and dropped it in a heap. He didn't care that his hands and jacket sleeves were smeared with blood and gray matter.

"Where are your keys, Dale? You're not gonna be needing 'em." He dug around inside his victim's pants pocket and found the key. He unlocked the van's cargo door and hoisted the body into the back, dropping it like a sack of rotten potatoes. Finally, he kicked fresh snow to cover the bloody tracks and turned his attention to the other vehicles in the parking lot.

He knew the Corolla belonged to James Carrier, so the Ranger must be Ryder's. He used his knife to force open the door. A search of the glove compartment revealed the vehicle's registration papers, which confirmed Chris as the owner and included his address, which Ray duly noted. He continued rifling through the compartment and a photograph of a young girl caught his attention. *My oh my, look what I've found.* Grinning, he shoved the photo in his pocket and considered the possibilities of what he could do with his discovery. His last act at the Ranger was puncturing its tires.

Then he took in his surroundings. He had paid an earlier visit to the gas station across from the park entrance, but it had closed early because of the blizzard, and he had parked his Cherokee behind the store. Now it was just a matter of waiting for his next target—Chris Ryder. *Sooner or later, you're gonna have to come through here, and I'll be waiting.*

# SEVEN

*Tuesday, February 7, 5:24 p.m.*

The sound of a gunshot blasting through the woods jolted Chris. His fear was matched by his confusion. *Who's shooting whom?* Ray was after him—this alone was enough to almost make him piss his pants—but was there someone else? *Are they fighting over me, like I'm some kind of prize?*

No matter how hard he tried to reassure himself that he would be okay, he knew that on the trail was a man whose sole objective was to kill him. Chris' objective was to stay alive—nothing else mattered. But deep down he knew that this wasn't true, that everything mattered. *There's nothing like the threat of death to bring life into focus.* He didn't want his life to end this way. There were far too many things left unfinished. At the top of that list was his relationship with Ann Marie. He yearned to see his daughter again. He longed to be present for her birthdays, for Christmases, for road trips, and every day in between. Thoughts of Ann Marie filled Chris with a renewed energy and purpose. *I will survive this.*

His best chance for survival lay a few minutes ahead of him at the cabin, and he continued on, ignoring the pain in his tired, wet, aching body.

He finally saw the rough outline of the cabin. *Yes!* He pumped his fist in the air, knowing he would be safe for the night.

Chris opened the battered door, stepped inside, and let his eyes adjust to the darkness around him. The air was cold, but the dilapidated shack would provide shelter against the snow, which was now turning to hard rain. He rested his tired body on a wooden chair, wishing he had a flashlight or matches and thinking back wistfully to his formative years spent in Boy Scouts. *They sure as hell didn't mention anything about being hunted during the winter in the middle of the woods.* But he was relieved nonetheless that he'd found shelter for the night. *With any luck, no one will find this place in the dark.*

Chris thought back to the grotesque image of the body on the trail. He felt guilt for celebrating victory in surviving death when this man had been mercilessly cut down. He also felt an overwhelming rage at the senseless injustice that had been perpetrated against the man. *But what can I do?* He struggled to decide his next move. If he stayed at the cabin until daylight, he could make his way to safety. But then a ruthless killer would escape capture. He was tired of hearing about criminals eluding justice. He had grown weary of hearing about gangland drive-by shootings, of victims paying the price while criminals manipulated the legal system. More than anything, he was tired of feeling powerless to stop them. *I have to try. I couldn't live with myself if I turned my back on him and let his killer walk.* He knew what he had to do. He stepped outside the cabin into the cold, dark night, and started his slog toward the park's entrance.

His thoughts turned to Ray Owens. To survive a killer like Ray, he would have to think like one. He was at once amazed and disturbed at how naturally this came to him now.

Ray would be waiting for him near the park entrance. He would have disabled his truck, somehow broken in and scavenged through the glove compartment. *Oh my God, Ray will know my address.* Chris felt the blood rushing to his head as he pictured Ray rifling through his apartment. He didn't care about the material possessions Ray would plunder. *He's going to find out about Ann Marie! I have to stop Ray before he leaves the park.* Chris braced himself for the inevitable showdown. *This is going to get messy.*

He cautiously made his way along the trail. Branches looked eerily like fingers reaching out to grab him. With every step, he expected Ray to jump out to surprise him like a warped jack-in-the-box. He tried to work out how he was going to approach Ray. *Calling him out into the open is useless because the bastard's got a gun.* Regardless of which plan he contemplated, it all came back to the fact that Ray held a crucial advantage. He would be armed and waiting.

Chris had two things working in his own favour: his knowledge of the trails, and the dark. Deciding that a sneak attack gave him the best odds, he kicked snow from the soggy ground searching for a makeshift weapon. Locating a tree with sturdy low-lying branches, he used his strength to crack one free. Aware of the sound the snapping limb made, he dropped to the ground and listened for movement in the distance. He had not been heard. He ventured onwards with one slow step at a time, his ears straining to detect danger ahead. At this pace, he would arrive at the entrance within fifteen minutes.

The falling rain was turning the trail to slush, weighing down his shoes, but he remained oblivious to the discomfort.

At six feet in height and one hundred and eighty pounds of lean muscle, Chris believed he was stronger than Ray. He pinned his hopes on being smarter than him as well, on finding a way to disarm him. When he reached the crossroads area on the trail, he paused and made a last-minute decision to bury the cell phone under the brush several feet away from the wooden trail marker. He continued on his mission until finally, after an eternity, he could faintly see the parking lot ahead of him. His heart pounded in anticipation of what would either be his best move—or his last one. *Let's get this over with.* Summoning his energy for the impending battle, he took a deep breath and tightened his grip on his weapon.

At the clearing leading to the park entrance, Chris crouched to the ground under the cover of the trees, surveying his surroundings in search of Ray. He could see his truck and two other vehicles. The silver Corolla had been there when he had first entered the parking lot, and he figured it belonged to the body he had discovered. The white van must have arrived after him and either belonged to Ray or had some connection to the shooting he'd heard earlier. "Where the hell are you, Ray?" he whispered.

Ray must be waiting for him somewhere nearby. Chris looked toward the gas station across the street from the park entrance, where he guessed Ray would have positioned himself to counter his attempts to get to his truck or make a run for the store. That brought their positions perilously close to each other. He shuddered. *What the hell do I do now?* His thought was interrupted by the involuntary grunt he let out as a piercing pain erupted in his right shoulder. The bullet had arrived without warning, and the shock of being shot left him slow to react.

"Bullseye. How does that feel, Ryder?" In what seemed like an instant, Ray emerged with a rifle and flashlight in his hands, looking down at Chris—the hunter sizing up his quarry.

Chris winced as he tried to sit up. He clutched his shoulder with his left hand, watching helplessly as blood seeped through his fingers and spread along the yellow sleeve of his jacket. "Ray—"

"What's wrong? Cat got your tongue?" Ray chortled. "That's only a graze. Nothing compared to what I'm gonna do. But first things first. Where's my phone?"

"I don't..." Chris grimaced as pain shot through his shoulder like shards of glass. "I don't have it."

"What the fuck do you mean, you don't have it?" Ray grabbed Chris by the collar of his jacket and dragged him to his feet. He checked Chris' pockets and, coming up empty, slammed him to the ground. Chris landed on his injured shoulder, sending fresh pain screaming through his body.

"Where is it, Ryder? You're starting to piss me off."

Chris summoned the strength to say, "I hid it. You kill me, you'll never get it back."

"Oh, I'll get it back. By the time I'm done with you, you'll be begging for a bullet, but I ain't gonna let you off that easy. I'm gonna have fun taking my time with you." He reached into his pocket, pulled out a picture, and shoved it in Chris' face. "Look what I found in your truck. Recognize this pretty young thing? I think she's got your eyes."

Chris' eyes bulged at the sight of Ann Marie's picture. "You leave her out of this, you hear me!" he raged.

"Or what, Ryder? What the fuck are you going to do about

it?" He aimed the rifle at Chris' head. "One shot, and it's over for you, and I'll still go after the girl."

Chris' will to fight was crushed. He swallowed dryly. "I'll take you to your phone, Ray."

# EIGHT

*Tuesday, February 7, 5:57 p.m.*

"911, what is your emergency?"

"My name is Deanna Ryder. I think my husband is trapped in Woodland Park."

"When was your last contact?"

"About an hour ago. He called me from the park and said he would be coming to my house. But he hasn't shown up, hasn't called, and I can't reach him."

"Is there anywhere else he may have gone?"

"No. He was coming over here to see our daughter. This isn't like him to not show up or call. I'm worried he got caught out there in the park with this weather. Can you do something?"

"I'm sorry, Mrs. Ryder. We can't initiate a missing person alert until twenty-four hours have—"

"But he could be hurt!"

"I understand your concern, ma'am. What I can do is provide you with the number for your local Search and Rescue agency. They'll want to know what your husband looks like, what he may have been wearing, and the kind of vehicle he drives, okay? Please hold for that number."

# NINE

The crows were back. Human movement on the trail had disrupted their roosting area. Chris wondered if they'd been there the whole time, watching quietly from their perches in the trees. Now they appeared restless, with their noisy chatter and frequent swooping from branch to branch, jockeying for the best view of the action unfolding beneath them. He remembered his Boy Scout leader telling him that a collection of crows is called a murder. *They've come to the right place.* Excruciating pain radiated from his shoulder. Even pain was no match for the way he felt as he walked with Ray to the phone's hiding place. *How could I have been so stupid to think I could beat him?*

"You know, Ryder, I'm beginning to like this place. Yeah, I think I'll come back here one day and check out an old cabin I heard about. But I won't forget you, Ryder. We'll always have this trail to remember."

Chris cursed under his breath. He wasn't going to be

beaten without putting up a fight. He had underestimated Ray, and now he hoped Ray would make the mistake of underestimating him.

"Hey, Ray, you really messed up, didn't you?"

"What the fuck are you talking about?" He gave Chris a puzzled look.

"I mean, what kind of professional killer, and I use the word 'professional' loosely here, loses his cell phone? Does your boss know you messed up?"

"I didn't mess up. Shit happens, and I deal with it. Just like I'm dealing with you."

"Seems like shit happens a lot around you, Ray."

Ray's face turned red, and he shoved Chris to the ground. "I could waste you right here." Without warning, he struck the barrel of the rifle against Chris' forehead, breaking the skin and sending a streak of blood down his cheek. He aimed the rifle in front of Chris' eyes, forcing him to look through the barrel of the gun. "I could put a hole right through your head right now, mess up your pretty face. How about I send your pretty young thing a picture of her daddy with a hole in his head?"

Chris knew he was getting to Ray and also that he had to ignore the pain burning through his body. He had to act now. "You sure you wouldn't mess that up too?"

Ray's eyes widened in blind rage. He swung his rifle over his head aiming to crack Chris' skull. This time, however, Chris rolled out of range and ducked the blow. He kicked Ray's leg, knocking him off balance and onto his back on the soggy ground. Chris pounced on top of Ray and punched him hard in the face.

"I'm gonna fucking kill you!" Ray raged, wiping blood

from his nose. The acrid smell of stale tobacco wafted towards Chris. Ray motioned to raise his gun, but Chris wrestled it from his hand and got back on his feet.

"I don't think so. Now it's my turn." He towered above Ray with the rifle pointed at his head. "Don't move."

"Go ahead, asshole. Do it. You don't have the balls to pull the trigger, Ryder."

"You have no idea what I want to do to you, Ray." *Do it. Do it.* A clamouring voice deep inside Chris' mind urged him to pull the trigger.

"Wanting and doing are two different things," Ray snarled.

"Don't push it."

"Your problem, Ryder, is you think too much. I don't give it a second thought. Killing is like breathing to me—comes natural. Like eating, shitting, and fucking."

"Like the way you killed the old man, Dobbin?" Chris spat.

"Who the fuck is that?"

"Your landlord. He didn't deserve to die."

"Why are you harping about that? That was years ago. Move on, Ryder. I have."

"You really don't get it, do you?" Chris shook his head in exasperation. "You killed a helpless man because you were disturbing the peace."

"Don't you talk to me about disturbing the goddamned peace. My peace was disturbed when that stupid cripple had the gall to knock on my door. He got what he deserved, and so will you."

Chris knew Ray was beyond reasoning, but he couldn't resist attempting to understand him. "Why did you kill the guy on the trail?"

"That was business, pure and simple." Ray's matter-of-fact tone made Chris queasy. "But killing you is gonna be pleasure. So, what you gonna do, Ryder? I ain't about to waltz with you to the pigs."

"That's exactly what you're going to do. Get up."

Ray pressed his hands against the slushy ground in a motion to stand to his feet. In a sudden move he threw slush in Chris' face and lunged at him. They struggled for control of the weapon and in the ensuing chaos, the rifle went off and a body collapsed to the ground.

# TEN

*Tuesday, February 7, 7:03 p.m.*

A team of Search and Rescue volunteers converged upon the Woodland Park entrance in response to Deanna Ryder's report.

"Mike, Ryder's truck's here. The tires have been flattened. Looks like someone punctured them."

A second volunteer inspecting a white Chevy van suddenly exclaimed, "Shit. Looks like blood smeared on the door handle."

"Over here," the third volunteer called. "There's footprints leading to the trail. And blood. We'd better—" The sound of a gunshot roared in the distance. "Fuck! I'm calling it in," the commander screamed. He dialed 911 and shouted, "Shots fired at Woodland Park!"

# ELEVEN

*Wednesday, February 8, 9:33 a.m.*

"Is he going to be okay?" Deanna asked the attending physician. She had received the call from the Health Sciences Center in the early hours of the morning, but they had suggested she visit once Chris regained consciousness. After a sleepless night, Deanna informed her bank manager that she would not be working and the school that her daughter would also be away, and rushed to the hospital.

The physician reviewed his patient's chart and looked at Deanna. "All things considered, I would say he's doing pretty well. He's a fighter and quite fortunate his wounds were not more severe. The bullet grazed his shoulder, and he sustained what looks to be a mild concussion."

"Can I see him?" Her voice quavered.

"That's fine by me, but right now he's being interviewed by the police."

"Mr. Ryder, my name is Sergeant Brandon Ryan. I'm with the RCMP Major Crimes Unit." The officer extended a powerful arm for a handshake, a symbolic gesture as he could see that with his arm in a sling, Chris wouldn't be shaking hands any time soon.

"I regret talking with you under these circumstances, but I have a few questions I'd like to ask you. If you're feeling up for that right now, of course."

Chris felt dazed. The Royal Canadian Mounted Police had found him unconscious on the trail and had taken him to the hospital. Spaced out on the Demerol the doctors had given him for the pain, he was having trouble concentrating on what the sergeant was saying, or recalling the reality of his ordeal.

He felt the blood drain from his face as one memory bubbled to the surface. "You've got to stop him. He's going to go after my family!"

"It's okay, Mr. Ryder," the sergeant said in a calm voice. "Your wife and daughter are fine. They're waiting outside."

"Where's Ray Owens?"

"I'm hoping you can help me with that one. Search and Rescue heard a shot and called us, but this Ray Owens you mention was gone before we arrived, and Search and Rescue didn't see anyone. It looks like he may have been parked at the gas station across the street from the entrance." He paused to make sure that Chris was following. "We're dealing with two bodies in Woodland Park, and I'm hoping you can help shed some light on this. Starting with this Owens fellow."

Chris' breathing accelerated in full-blown panic as he tried desperately to get up from his hospital bed. His weakened body betrayed him, and he lay back in frustration. "You've got to get him! I know he's going to go after my family."

"We'll get him," Sergeant Ryan said in a quietly confident tone. "But I'm going to need your help. I need to know everything you know about Ray Owens."

Chris told the sergeant about the cell phone he'd found on the trail, along with his history with Ray Owens. Sergeant Ryan took notes and occasionally asked questions for clarification and elaboration of details.

Even in his foggy state, Chris detected a slight accent of the East Coast, most likely Newfoundland. The sergeant's buzzcut and crewneck sweater gave him a military look. A faint scar above his eye slanting down towards his cheekbone told Chris that the sergeant had seen his share of adversity.

"We need to find that cell phone. It's a critical piece of evidence that might lead us to Ray Owens and his associate. Thank you for giving me the general location. I'll check it out."

Chris shook his head in disgust at himself. "I can't believe I actually thought I could go up against him."

Sergeant Ryan put his notepad away. "Mr. Ryder—"

"You can call me Chris."

"Okay, Chris. You know we're likely dealing with a man who kills people for a living?"

Chris thought he was about to be lectured with the "leave the bad guys for the cops" routine. "Yeah. I know I was stupid to go after him."

"Actually, what I was going to say was that your instincts and resourcefulness are likely what kept you alive."

"Thanks." Chris was pleasantly surprised, but his mood quickly turned to concern. "I know he's going to come at me again," he told the sergeant. "It's some kind of sick game to him."

"Well then, we'll have to work together to make sure that doesn't happen." The sergeant looked at Chris' shoulder sling. "You're in no shape to look after yourself right now. Are you going to be staying with your wife? Sorry, you said you're separated, right?"

"Yeah, we're separated. And that's an interesting question. After what I've put her through, I may need police protection—from her." Chris smiled.

"Well, we'll be assigning an officer to you and your family until this Owens guy is in custody." The sergeant reached into his pocket and handed Chris a business card. "Call me when you're being released so we can work out the details."

"Thank you, Sergeant."

"Call me Brandon."

"Thanks, Brandon."

"Your wife has been waiting anxiously to talk with you. I'll let her in. We'll talk again soon."

Chris braced himself for Deanna's visit. He knew she'd be concerned about him and figured he'd get some sympathy from her. It was hearing her tell him "I told you so" that he feared would do him in. Seeing the toll his work was taking on him and on their relationship, Deanna had been insisting for the last couple of years that he change his job. But never could he have imagined living through the events of the past twenty-four hours. What had taken place still felt surreal. But the implications for his family if Ray was targeting them were all too real.

The door to his room opened slowly, and Deanna

cautiously poked her head inside, unsure what she was going to see on the other side. Her normally lustrous chestnut hair was unkempt and her face drawn. Her reddened eyes finally made contact with Chris, and for an instant, it looked as if she didn't know what to say. She just kept staring. The silence quickly ended with her gasping, "Oh my God. What did he do to you?"

"I'm sorry, Dee." Chris tried to maintain his composure, to downplay the gravity of the situation. But his emotions abandoned him, and he could feel tears welling up in his eyes. "I never meant for this to happen. I swear to God, I won't let him touch you or Ann."

"When they told me what happened, I thought for sure we'd lost you," Deanna cried.

"It's going to be okay, Dee. I promise." Suddenly he panicked. "Where's Ann?"

"She's waiting outside. I wanted to see you first for myself. I had no idea what kind of shape you were going to be in." Deanna wiped her eyes.

"Does she know what happened?"

"I had to say something. It was kind of obvious something was wrong." She swiped the crumpled tissue across her face.

"I'm sorry. I know that's all I seem to say these days and I'm sick of it. It's going to change, Dee. I know I can't go on this way."

"*We* can't go on this way. We just can't."

"I know." He looked away from Deanna, too weary to fight.

Deanna took a deep breath and stared at Chris' hospital bed. "Well, I suppose you'll be staying with us for awhile."

"I can make other arrangements, Dee. I—"

"Oh, be quiet. You're coming home with us. Don't even think about staying anywhere else."

"You sure?"

"It's the first thing Ann Marie asked when I told her what happened. She wants you home. I've told her this doesn't mean we're getting back together. It's just until you're back on your feet."

Chris felt a lump in his throat. He was never one for public displays of emotion and could count on one hand the number of times he'd allowed himself to cry in the presence of another person. Yet now he was an emotional wreck.

"That means a lot to me, Dee." He wiped his eyes and took a deep breath, which quickly reminded him of his wounds. "I'd love to see Ann now."

# TWELVE

*Wednesday, February 8, 6:36 p.m.*

The bus stopped two blocks away from her parent's home, and Elizabeth Carrier hurried off. Her mother would not say over the phone what was wrong or why Elizabeth had to rush home from her night class at the University of British Columbia. But her mother had never before called during class, and Elizabeth could tell from her choked words that she'd been crying. Something was wrong—terribly wrong. *Is it Dad?* She realized she hadn't talked with her father in a few days, but that was not unusual. *Please, don't let it be Dad.* Dry-mouthed with fear, she quickened her pace and tried to avoid guessing what calamity had befallen her family.

It was dark, and the falling snow had turned to slush, emptying the streets of cars and people. All but one, Elizabeth noted. But as the driver exited his idling truck and started walking quickly towards her, her heart rate accelerated with panic. *Do I know him? Why is he approaching me?* She had no time to react, no time to scream, as she was struck in the head with a Maglite and knocked unconscious.

In one swift motion, Elizabeth's assailant grabbed her body before it hit the ground, threw her over his shoulder, and carried her to his truck. He hoisted her into the cab of the truck and drove off into the night.

# THIRTEEN

*Thursday, February 9, 9:09 a.m.*
The killing ground was littered with corpses on blood-red snow while riotous crows picked over human remains.

Chris was jarred awake by the disturbing images. His sheets were soaked with sweat, and it took a minute for him to remember where he was. When he got his bearings and realized he was no longer on the trail or in imminent danger, his anxiety gave way to relief. He was grateful that Deanna had taken another day off work to help him recover from his injuries, to say nothing of the infinite pleasure he felt each time Ann Marie raced into his room to check on him.

His ordeal had given him a new appreciation for life. He knew more than ever that his daughter was the most important part of his life and he would do everything in his power to keep Ann Marie and Deanna safe.

They were planning to go out for breakfast at Wilbur's, which in happier times had been a Ryder family tradition. While Ray continued to occupy a large part of his mind, Chris was looking forward to the family excursion. His thoughts of scrambled eggs and sausages waiting for him at the diner were interrupted by the ringing phone.

"Chris, it's Sergeant Ryan for you." Deanna brought him the phone from the kitchen.

"Hi, Sarge—uh, Brandon. What's new?"

"I hope I'm not calling too early this morning. I wanted to tell you before you hear it anywhere else."

"Tell me what? Is everything okay?" Chris felt his muscles tense.

"Depends. We arrested Ray Owens early this morning."

"Really?" Just hearing Ray's name made Chris lose his appetite for breakfast. "How did you find him?"

"Well, that's the thing. He walked straight into the detachment and gave himself up."

"Why the hell would he do that?"

"I was surprised myself. But in the end, it doesn't really matter. We've got him."

His queasiness increased, and Chris started to feel the room spinning out of control. In a last-ditch effort to prevent a fall, he propped himself against the wall. *What's Ray doing? He's got to have a plan.* He was relieved to know that Ray was no longer loose on the street, but he knew in his gut that Ray would never surrender his freedom and turn himself over to the authorities unless it was part of a larger plan. But what could the plan be?

Deanna, who had left to make final preparations for their outing, returned to the room. She could tell from Chris' body language that their lives were about to change yet again. "What's wrong, Chris?"

"It's okay, Dee. Everything's okay. I'll just be a minute."

But he didn't have the energy to keep up the act. He knew that their happy days were once again coming to a close.

"Chris, you still there?" Sergeant Ryan asked.

"I'm here. I'm sure Ray's got an angle. I just don't know what it is yet."

"Well, that's for you guys to find out."

"What do you mean?"

"Well, for starters, he's been talking about hearing voices. And he waived his right to a lawyer. Crown counsel has ordered a psychiatric assessment at IFP. That's where you work, isn't it?"

There it was, the angle Chris figured Ray was going after. "You said he's hearing voices?" Chris was sure it was an act, but forewarned was forearmed.

"He's saying there's a voice—Mr. Dobbin—telling him to do things, including the killings on the trail."

*Goddamnit, he's playing games with me.* Mr. Dobbin was not a voice in Ray's head; he was the landlord he had killed. Ray was orchestrating an admission to the hospital where Chris worked and was using Mr. Dobbin to rub Chris' nose in it.

Sergeant Ryan brought Chris back to the moment. "We haven't been able to locate the cell phone. We'll probably need you to go in there to give us a hand to find it. It's just too vast a space. Are you up for that?"

"I guess I'll have to be." It was the last place he wanted to revisit after everything he'd been through.

"There's something else, Chris. There's a young woman named Elizabeth Carrier. She's the eighteen-year-old daughter of the victim in Woodland Park, James Carrier. Her family has lost contact with her. She's not officially considered missing yet, as it's been less than twenty-four hours, but given what happened to her father, we're not taking any chances. We're holding a press conference later today to appeal to the public to come forward with any information about Elizabeth."

"You think Ray is connected with her disappearance?"

"From the way he's been acting, I think he's guilty as sin, but we need evidence. Listen, I shouldn't be telling you all of this, but I know what you went through and I don't think it's over yet."

"What do you mean?"

"We've questioned Owens, but he's been pretty cagey with us. He's given us absolutely nothing. He keeps talking about you. Chris, you'd better be careful around him."

*When am I ever going to be free from this bastard?* "I think he's playing games."

"You might be right. He could be having fun at our expense. Chris, if he really does have something to do with Elizabeth Carrier, you may be the best chance we have in discovering what that something is. He seems to feel some bizarre connection to you. We need to use that to our advantage."

Chris had hoped that Ray's arrest would mean the end of their association with each other. But he now knew that their involvement was far from over and that their fates were inextricably bound together. He felt a heavy burden settle on his shoulders. "I'll do my best."

# FOURTEEN

*Thursday, February 9, 9:09 a.m.*

Ray lay stretched out on a filthy, stinking mattress in a police cell looking at the shit-smeared ceiling above him and admiring the job he'd done. He figured it would help make a convincing argument for a psychiatric evaluation at the shithole IFP. In fact, he was counting on it.

He was feeling uncharacteristically edgy. Chris Ryder had that effect on him. Until Ryder had entered his life, no one had ever been able to get a rise out of Ray, a fact that he'd held as a point of pride. Ryder got to him, and it pissed him off royally.

He knew he could have continued his run from the police. He had no problem with that. But it was Ryder who was responsible for putting him on the run. *That* was a problem in Ray's mind. *There's no way I'm running from Ryder.* He'd make Ryder pay for what he'd done to him. He had big plans for Chris Ryder. *He's going to wish he'd killed me when he had the chance.*

# FIFTEEN

*Thursday, February 9, 10:39 a.m.*

After his phone call from Sergeant Ryan, Chris accompanied Deanna and Ann Marie to breakfast, but all he could stomach was three cups of black coffee. He replayed the conversation he'd had with the sergeant, as Ann Marie chattered on joyously about her current favourite movie, *Princess Ariana.* Deanna attempted to talk with him about plans for the week ahead, including Ann Marie's swimming and dance lessons, but he kept zoning out. When they returned home and their daughter was happily playing in her room, Deanna confronted Chris in the living room. "This can't go on."

"What do you mean? Didn't we have a good time today?"

"Oh, come off it, Chris. You bloody well know what I'm talking about. After your phone call from the police, your thoughts were a million miles from us. It's not fair to Ann Marie or to me."

"I'm trying, Dee. I really am."

Deanna shook her head. "I'm sure you are, but I feel like

we're right back to square one. Your work takes priority over everything else in your life, including our daughter and me. You won't let me help you. You're still shutting me out."

"I don't talk about work with you because it's better if I try to keep it away, separate from us. And in case you didn't notice, this is about more than *just* work. A guy tried to kill me!"

"I *do* know how serious this is, Chris, but you're avoiding the issue. We've been through this before. Remember what the therapist said: 'You compartmentalize.' That's the problem. It doesn't work. You end up blocking us out. I can't take it any more." Her voice became throaty as she fought off tears.

"So, what are you saying, Dee? You want me to leave?" His face was getting hot with frustration. He hated to see Deanna cry, and hated being the cause of her sorrow. "I'm sorry." He looked away from her.

"I know, Chris. Maybe a small part of both of us thought this time would be different. But it isn't, and it's for the best that we separated." They both remained silent for a moment.

Chris broke the awkward silence. "How do you want to do this?"

"Let's tell her at supper. And Chris, I don't *want* to do this at all. I know you love Ann Marie, and she loves you. She'll understand. We all just need time to—"

Shaking his head, Chris could do no better than to mutter, "I need to make some calls," and left the room.

Apart from a pout and a sad little "Oh, Daddy," Ann Marie took the news fairly well that her father would be moving back to his apartment. Her parents took great pains to present a positive rationale for the move. They decided to break the news as she was devouring her dessert, vanilla ice cream topped with chocolate sauce. After supper, they shopped for groceries, and Deanna dropped Chris off at his apartment. His truck had been towed from Woodland Park to his apartment building after the police had finished collecting evidence and the slashed tires had been replaced.

Once Ann Marie and Deanna had left, Chris packed away his groceries. He glanced around the sparse, uninviting bachelor unit, hastily chosen out of necessity after he and Deanna had separated. Other than a bed and a futon couch, the apartment was unfurnished, with the notable exception of a family portrait taken during happier times, hanging on the living room wall. Chris' only extravagance was the Bose sound dock for his iPod, which lay next to his outdated television.

He switched on his television—and nearly dropped the remote when he realized he was watching highlights of an earlier press conference covering the arrest of Ray Owens in what the media had dubbed the "murder at Woodland Park." He didn't recognize the officer identified as the lead investigator who was doing the majority of the talking, but he could see Sergeant Ryan standing next to him.

The newsclip cut to a statement from James Carrier's brother, who expressed appreciation to the police in apprehending the killer. His voice trembled as he pleaded for the public's help in coming forward with any information about Elizabeth Carrier. A photograph of a beautiful young woman with blonde hair and blue eyes appeared on the television screen. Next came footage of Ray Owens being escorted in handcuffs from a police car into the courthouse, where he was formally charged with several offences, including the attempted murder of a social worker from the Institute of Forensic Psychiatry. The reporter summarized Ray's previous admission at IFP accompanied by file footage of the Institute.

Only now did Chris realize that his private tribulations involving Ray Owens had become front-page headlines. It was an irresistibly sensationalistic story: a man who had murdered a defenceless senior and, after a questionable early release from prison, went on to kill two more people. The fact that he had attempted to kill his former social worker and was now suspected of having some connection with the disappearance of the daughter of one of his victims meant that for the foreseeable future, audiences would be riveted by any news about Ray Owens.

Chris figured the administration at IFP would be in damage-control mode over his connection with Ray and the so-called "murder at Woodland Park." He realized that his manager, David Evans, would not be in his office at this hour but still phoned and left him a message to discuss returning to work. Next, he called his own office number to retrieve his work voicemail. His heart hammered as he listened to a disturbing message from David that both he and Chris' director wanted to see him the following day, and that David had scheduled Chris for a critical-incident debriefing interview for the next day.

He wasn't surprised about the debriefing. While the incident with Ray hadn't occurred in the workplace, it had involved a former patient who was about to be re-admitted to IFP. The administration would insist Chris discuss with a counselor what had happened in Woodland Park. And he knew he would probably need to jump through several hoops before he would be considered well enough to return to work. What did surprise him, however, was the name of the psychologist conducting the interview—Stephanie Rowe.

# SIXTEEN

*Friday, February 10, 7:09 a.m.*

Chris woke from another spate of torturous nightmares of James Carrier's body, covered in blood with his torso blown apart. He had gone to bed late hoping that fatigue would set in and force his body into slumber. But the images and worries bashing away inside his head kept him wide awake into the early hours of the morning.

He prepared for his interview, acutely aware of his nerves, as nausea and a headache destroyed his appetite for breakfast. He was willing to bet that the CBC had a camera crew camped out in the IFP parking lot, hoping to get the latest update on Ray, and he was sure this would not win him any favours with his director.

Chris was even more anxious about seeing Stephanie again. They had known each other for the better part of a decade. Throughout much of that time, there was a strong mutual attraction between them. But they were victims of bad timing: when Chris first fell hopelessly in love with Stephanie, she was engaged. That engagement broke off, but by the time she re-entered his life some years later, Chris was married to Deanna. Happily married, he thought wistfully, but when he was being truthful with himself, he knew that while his marriage had been many things, happy was not one of them. In recent months, he had come to look back upon his marriage with Deanna as another case of bad timing on both their parts. But he refused to allow himself to focus on regrets because he knew Ann Marie was the amazing result of their union.

Chris had last seen Stephanie three years ago on the eve of her transfer to the West Coast Federal Correctional Center, where she had accepted a position as a behavioural consultant in the psychology department. He had recently heard that she was taking on brief contract work at IFP but he had not yet run into her. He couldn't help but wonder why she had offered to conduct the critical-incident debriefing with him. His pulse quickened as he drove into the IFP parking lot.

The Institute of Forensic Psychiatry stood as a state-of-the-art, two-hundred-bed facility, providing court-ordered psychiatric assessments as well as treatment for men and women with mental health problems who had come into conflict with the criminal justice system. When Chris had last come to work, Ray Owens had been a distant memory. Now he couldn't get rid of him. He also knew that given the public nature of his recent ordeal, he would be on display at work, with people scrutinizing his every move.

He made his way to the reception office, dominated by a brawny security officer. "Hey, Horace. How're ya doing?"

"Holy Jesus, Chris, I've been reading all about you. Sorry to hear what happened, man."

"Yeah, well, what can you do?" Chris got along well

with Horace. They shared an interest in hockey and often commiserated over the Vancouver Canucks' trials and tribulations. To say that Horace was a fan of the Canucks would be an understatement—his Honda Civic hatchback was completely adorned in the team's signature blue, green, silver, and white. Chris knew Horace wanted to talk about his misadventures at Woodland Park, but he wasn't feeling up to it. Instead, he waved goodbye and walked through the door towards the psychology department, where his interview was to take place.

As he approached the office, Chris took a deep breath and glanced at his watch. Realizing he was ten minutes early, he stood motionless, deliberating whether to announce his arrival or wait a few more minutes before knocking on the door. While he hesitated, the door opened and there stood Stephanie, a look of confusion on her face.

"Oh, hi, Stephanie." *Real smooth, Ryder,* Chris scolded himself.

"Hi, Chris. Have you been waiting long?"

"No. I just got here. I... uh... was about to knock when you opened. So, how are you doing?" He was nervous and hot as hell, and wished he had worn a lighter shirt. Most of all, he was struck by how beautiful Stephanie looked.

"I'm well. Come in." She stood back from the doorway. "It's been a while, hasn't it?"

"Yeah, I guess it's been about three years?" Stephanie's auburn hair was styled differently from how he remembered it, and the years had been good to her. Chris wondered which New Age fitness craze she was doing to keep her body toned, and immediately felt his cheeks flush with embarrassment.

"Chris, I'm very sorry to hear what happened. When the

referral came to our office, I was assigned to take it. I hope that's okay with you."

"Sure, yeah, that's fine. I mean, somebody has to do it, right?" He was taken aback by Stephanie's business-as-usual demeanour, but just like old times, he found he couldn't read her.

"All right then. Let's get started. You understand that your participation in this meeting is voluntary and that my role is to provide support and not treatment, yes?" Chris nodded his head in agreement, although he doubted he'd describe his participation as truly voluntary. *More like voluntold.* "The content of our discussion will remain confidential." She handed Chris a consent form to review. Once he had signed it, they started.

Chris summarized what had happened on the trail, as well as his previous history with Ray Owens. Stephanie listened, took the occasional note, and asked how he was sleeping, eating, and concentrating. He was becoming more and more annoyed with the increasing frequency with which she kept asking him, "Can you please elaborate?" He also realized he had underestimated the intensity of what was being asked of him. He found it difficult to analyze how he had felt when he discovered the body and when he was forced to look through the barrel of Ray's rifle. Stephanie, adept at picking up on his long pauses and apparent struggles, placed her notebook on the table.

"Let's slow things down a bit and go over again why we're here today."

"I know why I'm here, Stephanie."

"All right, tell me your understanding of why you're here?"

Chris bowed his head and sighed, a move he knew Deanna always called his "here we go again" move. "For Christ's sake, you know the kind of work I do. Give me a break. Don't you think I know what you're getting at? I experienced a traumatic event as you like to say. So people want to make sure I'm not experiencing PTSD. That I'm not going to flip out on someone at work. I know your questions are standard procedure and that's why I'm here, but I'm telling you I'm okay."

"I'll tell you what concerns me. We've been here..." Stephanie glanced at her watch. "...forty minutes, and I have yet to hear you say in real, specific terms what happened to you on that trail. In my opinion, you are avoiding acknowledging that you were shot. That a man almost killed you. That's a common—"

"Well, that's pretty obvious, isn't it?" Chris interrupted, a sarcastic note in his voice.

"What's obvious?"

He was angry now. "That some bastard tried to kill me. It's not like I'm the first guy this has happened to."

Stephanie paused briefly. "Look, Chris, there are two things about what you just said that interest me. First, you're right. You're not the first person to survive being shot. But that doesn't make it any less traumatic. Second, you said 'some bastard,' which implies that you didn't know your attacker. But you knew your attacker—Ray Owens. A former patient of yours tried to kill you. Now, this same 'bastard' is going to be coming to your workplace, where you'll come into contact with each other. So that makes me wonder how ready you are to return to work and how ready you are to see Ray Owens again, when you haven't even said his name out loud."

Stephanie took a deep breath before saying in a softer,

lower voice, "The point I'm getting at, Chris, is that all of your reactions today are normal, given what you went through. But it's important to acknowledge them, to talk about them. Or your future actions and reactions to everyday occurrences run the risk of not being normal."

Now it was Chris who paused, looking for the most diplomatic way to get his point across. "Listen, Stephanie. I know what you're saying. I understand that—I really do."

"So why are you being so resistant?"

"*You* need to understand something, too. Some people feel better by talking about things. That's fine—good for them. But I'm not one of those people. I have other ways of dealing with stuff, you know."

"Good. Such as?"

"Such as... working it out in my own head. Running. I don't know, but I know what the problem is and I know I have to solve it on my own. I just do better on my own with this stuff, and I'm getting tired of hearing people say I need to open up—be *emotionally available*. Jesus."

Stephanie looked confused. "Are you talking about your marriage now?"

Chris was annoyed by Stephanie's question. "What does it matter what I'm talking about? What I'm saying is, whether it's you or it's a marriage counselor, or... hell... freakin' Dr. Phil. I know what I need and don't need. And I don't need to be told that I need to talk about my marriage and my mother and my early childhood experiences and on and on and on. I don't need that."

"Yet it was you who brought up your mother, not me."

"Yeah, but sooner or later, I know that's where it's headed. It always is."

"So why do you think it always goes back to your mother, Chris?"

Chris fell silent. He felt exhausted. His sleepless nights and restless days were catching up to him. He felt he had no energy to argue any longer. He hadn't expected this.

Stephanie seemed to sense Chris was shutting down and let him off the hook. "We've done a lot of talking here this morning," she said, "so perhaps we should wind things down for today. I would like to end by sharing some information with you. What you do with this information is entirely up to you. You mentioned PTSD earlier, and I think it may be worthwhile to briefly review some of the common signs and symptoms."

"So you think I have PTSD. What a shocker." He paused, thinking about what he had said. "Sorry, that came out wrong. I don't mean to be a jerk, Stephanie. I'm interested. Go on."

"Sorry if I sound like a textbook, but common signs to watch for in post-traumatic stress disorder include recurring and intrusive images, thoughts, or feelings about the trauma— in your case, about what you experienced on the trail. Some people experience distressing dreams or a sense that they are reliving the experience." She let that sink in for a moment before going on. "Avoidance symptoms are also common, where efforts are taken to avoid the thoughts and feelings associated with the trauma. Or avoiding activities, places, or people who may be reminders of the trauma. Does any of this sound familiar?"

Chris felt his cheeks flush. "Not really," he said.

"Other symptoms can include anxiety and difficulty falling or staying asleep, difficulty concentrating, irritability, or outbursts of anger. But I'm sure this wouldn't apply to you," she said playfully. "Seriously, I think it's important for you to keep an open mind and a watchful eye for these symptoms. Okay?"

"Sure." Chris quickly tried to change the topic. "So tell me, do you think I'm ready to go back to work?"

"Do you *feel* ready?"

"Well, I do need to get paid. So what do you think?"

Stephanie took a long pause, and Chris could tell from her slight frown that he was not going to like her response. "What I think is that you should see someone at the Employee Assistance Program, given the traumatic experience you had. EAP will be able to—"

"Oh come on, Stephanie, is that really necessary?"

"You asked for my opinion, and I gave it to you. Critical-incident debriefing is not designed for treatment, whereas someone at EAP could assist you in that area if warranted. I think it would be good for you to talk to someone there."

Chris deliberated on her suggestion, massaging his fingers against his forehead in a feeble effort to ward off his looming headache. "Stephanie, I don't want to go to a bunch of counseling sessions at EAP, only to be told what I already know—that I experienced a traumatic event and that I have to look after myself. I know all this, I know that I'm going to be fine. Couldn't I just see you a few times? And I promise, if after that you still think I need counseling, I'll check out the EAP. What do you say?" Chris gave a nervous smile.

Stephanie paused. Their eyes briefly locked, and she shyly looked away. Finally, she said, "This is not how we normally practice, but I suppose we could schedule a follow-up meeting after your first day back to work, to see how it went."

Chris sighed with relief. "Sure. What time?"

"Call me tomorrow once you know what your schedule looks like, and we can go from there. I understand you have a meeting with David?"

"Yeah. Actually, I have a meeting with him *and* Florence in about an hour. Hey, at least I can tell him the great news that I'm coming back," he said, making an attempt at humour. "And Stephanie, I'm sorry about earlier."

"Like I said, given the circumstances, this is to be expected. See you soon." Stephanie opened her office door. He wanted to say more, but didn't know what to say, or how to say it. His exit felt as awkward as his entry.

# SEVENTEEN

*Friday, February 10, 10:04 a.m.*

An hour to kill before his meeting with his manager and director, and Chris was anxious to get it over and done with. It wasn't his manager who concerned him. He had great respect for David Evans and knew him to be compassionate and fair. What worried Chris was meeting with Florence Threader, an effective and efficient director who had served as an administrator at IFP for as long as he could remember. Her dedication to the hospital was beyond question, and she demanded the same commitment from her staff.

Above all else, Florence Threader despised controversy. It seemed that every time IFP was in the news, it concerned some problem that Florence and a team of spin doctors had to resolve. Chris figured Florence wanted to ream him out over his recent "antics" that had placed IFP once again in the media spotlight. It wouldn't matter to her that he had hardly been a willing participant in his confrontation with Ray Owens.

To distract himself, he dropped in on his colleague,

psychiatrist Marilyn Stevenson. She was behind her desk, reviewing one of her court reports. He grinned at the sight of her wearing her "lucky suit," a well-tailored navy-blue business suit, which she reserved for days when she was in court. She appeared surprised to see him in her doorway.

"I didn't know you were coming in today, Chris. How are you?" she asked with a genuine tone of concern. "I've been so worried about you. I couldn't believe what happened."

"I'll survive." He smiled. "It's nice to see a pleasant face. I have a meeting with David and Florence in a little bit."

"Florence? Ouch. That can't be good, my friend."

"No kidding."

"She already met with me, Chris."

"Really?"

"She wanted me to go over my report on Owens from his last admission here three years ago. To make sure I didn't miss anything."

"That's confidence-building, isn't it?"

"You know he's coming back here, don't you? Ray Owens."

"Yeah, it's been hard to miss. He's all over the news—and loving every bit of the attention."

Marilyn nodded. "Florence also wanted to make sure that he gets assigned to me again for this admission. Despite my request for reassignment."

"Sorry to hear that, Marilyn."

"Well, the rationale is that I know him. And for the sake of continuity, I'm in the best position to complete the assessment as quickly as possible and ship him back to pre-trial where he'll wait for court."

"Lucky you."

"And Chris, just a heads-up. He won't be in a seclusion room. Despite my misgivings, he'll be on the unit with the other patients. He made several baseless complaints to the ombudsman during his last admission. So Florence has ordered that we start Ray out on the open unit until he gives us sufficient reason to seclude him from the other guys. Oh, and Florence also made it clear that she wants Gerald assigned as his social worker."

"Figures." Again Chris was feeling sick to his stomach, thinking how administration was coming down hard about this case. He felt particularly bad for Marilyn. Normally they worked together on court-ordered remand assignments. But he had already suspected he would not be working the Owens case, and that suited him just fine.

"Well, I'd better get going. If you hear that I've taken a special project in Timbuktu, you'll know I pissed them off."

Marilyn stopped him. "Look, Chris, I'm so sorry about all of this. If you ever want to talk, you know I'm here."

"I know, Marilyn. Thanks."

"There's talk, by the way, of having Ray declared a dangerous offender. If there's any silver lining to all you went through, it may be that you helped get that psychopath off the street for a very long time."

"We'll see." The news was cold comfort to him, given that the chaos Ray Owens had created in Chris' personal life was now spilling into his professional life.

Chris walked to the administration building and informed Gayle, the receptionist, that he had arrived for his appointment.

He was fifteen minutes early, but this was the kind of meeting where he dared not be even one minute late: Florence was infamous for publicly castigating people about their disregard for punctuality. He slipped into the washroom to relieve his dry mouth and try to calm his nerves before returning to the reception area.

Gayle told him Florence was ready to see him. Once inside her office, Chris saw his manager, David, sitting ramrod-straight and looking nervous. *I know the feeling*. He felt his collar tightening, like a noose, around his neck.

Seated behind a massive desk, Florence did not bother with niceties. "Chris, sit down, please."

"Thank you, Florence. Hello, David." *Be respectful and don't react to anything they throw at you, Ryder.*

Florence wasted no time in getting to her point. "I wanted to talk to you about the situation we're in. I'm sure you know what I'm talking about."

"I believe so." Chris loosened his collar.

"The Ray Owens *debacle*." Florence let the last word hang in the air, as her glare skewered Chris. Sweat trickled down from his armpits and he wondered whether it was visible to his director. "I'm sure you've been following the news. It's a damn media circus."

"I—"

"I do *not* want to hear your excuses." Florence stood and slammed her hands down on her desk. Chris had never shared such a small space with her before, and she was even more imposing and terrifying up close and personal. She was taller than he, as thin as a broomstick, and her words lashed out at him. "We were on the front page of the *Vancouver Sun* yesterday and again today. Not the kind of attention we need."

Impatience edged into her voice. "I read Dr. Stevenson's report from Ray Owens' last admission at IFP. Her opinion back then was that he was not acutely mentally ill, but had strong anti-social personality traits." She shook her head in utter frustration. "Someone like Owens is toxic to this entire system. We work so hard to demystify mental illness and fight negative stereotypes about the forensic psychiatric system. We try to educate the general public that our patients have an illness, and that contrary to what the media spit out, they're not all murderers. Then along comes Ray Owens, and the media glom on to him. He's going to set us back ten years."

Chris reflected on the media fascination with Ray. *If it bleeds, it leads.*

"Then there's the impact he's having on our patients and how they see themselves in the mirror. They're afraid to step outside with the frenzy that's brewing out there. On top of that, I've had the Minister of Health and the Attorney General on my back about Owens, and our communications department is working overtime in damage control. "So I want you to understand something, Chris—and understand it well. No one is happy right now."

"Florence, I—" Chris started, only to be cut off again by his director. He glanced over at David fidgeting uncomfortably in his chair.

"The *Sun* managed to get your picture, Chris. How did that happen?" She gave him a scorching look.

"I... I don't know," he stammered in surprise. He hadn't seen the morning paper, which for some reason hadn't been delivered to his door. And he certainly hadn't been aware of his picture being taken.

"Listen to me very carefully." Florence spoke very slowly

and precisely. "You are not, under any circumstances, to give any interviews. Is that clear?"

"Yes."

"Our communications department will handle that."

"I understand."

"Now, Ray Owens is being admitted to our hospital this afternoon, as I'm sure you know. The whole damn province seems to know."

"Yes, I was aware of that."

"I've made it clear that I want him assigned to Dr. Stevenson. She did the assessment during his last admission, and I want her doing this one."

Chris nodded. "Yes."

"I understand you usually work with Dr. Stevenson, correct?"

"Yes."

"Not this time. I do not want you anywhere near Owens. Is that clear?"

"Yes." Chris was wondering if he would get a chance to say anything in his defence.

"You cannot be seen to be in any way involved in his assessment, or there'll be accusations that we've got a conflict of interest. In fact, you are not to have any communication with him—whatsoever."

"I understand."

"I take it that you're feeling ready to return to work?"

Chris nodded. "I had a debriefing meeting earlier this morning."

"And your injuries are healing? I won't be hearing from WorkSafeBC, right?"

"Right. The—"

"Good. So let's put this behind us, and move on." Her dour face forced a smile, sending shivers down Chris' back.

"Okay."

Florence sat back down. "David, do you have anything to add?"

"No, not really, Florence. Other than to tell you, Chris, that Gerald will be assigned to work with Mr. Owens. Gerald will want to meet with you to pick up your old file, ask you some questions. In due course—"

"No," Florence interrupted angrily. "Not in due course. Today. Chris, you will meet with Gerald today. Give him the information he needs. Is that clear?"

"Yes, I'll contact Gerald after I leave here."

"Fine." Florence looked at Chris and David. "I do not want to have this conversation with either of you again. Have a good day." She dismissed them both.

Chris made a hasty retreat from her office, David close on his heels. Once outside, David gave Chris a don't-drag-me-down-with-you look and told him that he would be in contact with Stephanie Rowe about his progress. Then he left Chris alone to make sense of what had just happened. *Well, at least there's no special project in Timbuktu.... On the other hand, perhaps I'd be better off in Timbuktu about now.*

He made another washroom pit stop. He didn't need a mirror to know that he looked like hell. Lines were forming on his forehead, and his eyes were bloodshot from his sleepless nights, not to mention his facial bruising from Ray's assault. He splashed cool water on his face and could taste the residue of salt from his sweat. *This day just keeps getting better and better.* He'd endured a grilling from Stephanie and a torture session with his director. He still had to face the remand unit to meet with Gerald, and avoid Ray Owens at the same time. As Chris approached the entrance to the remand ward, he felt his heart hammer and his stomach flutter.

*I will survive this.*

As Chris approached Alpha unit, he thought back to his first day of orientation to IFP when his manager had described the unit and the remand process for him. "Alpha unit is a maximum-security twenty-bed remand ward for individuals charged with criminal offences ranging from mischief to murder. Male patients are admitted here for court-ordered psychiatric assessments. Chris, you need to know that there are two types of assessments. A Fitness assessment involves a psychiatrist's opinion of a patient's ability to understand the court process and his ability to communicate with counsel. An NCRMD assessment is the psychiatrist's opinion of the individual's mental state at the time that he had committed the alleged offence, and whether he could be considered not criminally responsible on account of a mental disorder."

Chris recalled David's patience in describing the remainder of the hospital to him. "The other units are designed for patients with other legal status. This includes those found NCRMD. Beta unit, for example, is a maximum security unit designated for inmates from provincial jails who require admission at IFP as a Temporary Absence in order to receive treatment under the *Mental Health Act*. The remaining units range from medium to minimum levels of security and a patient's admission on a unit is determined in part by their degree of mental and behavioural stability.

You'll be working as part of a multidisciplinary team which in addition to psychiatry and nursing, also includes psychology, occupational therapy, substance abuse counselors and case managers. And we have great vocational and rehabilitation staff, along with a teacher and chaplain."

Chris remembered his trepidation when he had first stepped onto Alpha unit. David had made him feel welcome by describing how, as a social worker, he factored into the remand process. "One of your jobs," he said, "is gathering collateral information from a patient's family and friends, particularly on how the patient was functioning at the time of the offence. This information will complement the interviews the psychiatrist will conduct with the patient. The psychiatrist's report is then presented to the judge when the patient attends court."

*I can't believe that was ten years ago.* Chris had worked with many patients since his orientation, and he'd collected collateral from a lot of family members. But Ray Owens had always stood out. Chris was not aware of any living Owens family members or close friends and acquaintances. In fact, he vividly remembered Ray being particularly sensitive about this topic—he became prickly upon hearing even general questions about his family. Chris had been intrigued enough to explore this topic further but was hindered by Ray's short stay.

As to Ray's present admission at IFP, Chris knew that the psychiatrist would be interested in Chris' observations of him from their time at Woodland Park. Dr. Stevenson would use this information to help her form an opinion as to whether Ray was suffering symptoms of mental illness when he committed his criminal acts on the trail or whether he could be considered criminally responsible.

The irony of the situation was not lost on Chris—that he wasn't the interviewer in this case but the interviewee. His colleague, Gerald Reed, would be the social worker assisting Dr. Stevenson with Ray's assessment. Chris had mentored Gerald on his arrival at the IFP social work department, and they'd worked well together ever since. Chris hoped Gerald's questions would be brief, so he could go home and put an end to this wretched day.

Hand trembling, he reached for his fob key to gain entry into the locked unit. On the other side awaited the man who had tried to kill him just a few days before, the man who had threatened his daughter. He took a deep breath, opened the door, and entered the unit. *That wasn't so bad.* He walked down the hallway towards the nursing station. Although Alpha unit was a maximum-security ward, the staff consisted of nurses and health-care professionals rather than correctional officers and guards.

Chris recognized Alex Dunbar, the head nurse in charge of the unit. After several years of working together at IFP, they'd developed a respect for each other, and Chris knew Alex to be strict but fair. At six feet two inches and two hundred and twenty pounds, Alex was an imposing figure, and few people disputed his authority.

"Hey, Alex, how's it going?" Chris called out.

Alex, who had been talking with his staff, stopped and gave a surprised look at Chris. "Damn. I didn't expect to see you back so soon. How the hell are you?"

"I'm here. That should count for something."

"Yeah. But why are you here? I heard you got banged up pretty bad." He looked Chris over as if searching for visual confirmation of his injuries.

"My shoulder is sore as hell, but I'll survive."

Mark, one of the other nurses, piped up, "I thought for sure they'd reassign you to another ward. You know he's here, don't you?"

"I know he's here." Chris wasn't surprised at the question, given that Mark was on the hospital's occupational safety and health committee. Chris knew there would be people who would think he was returning to work too soon, but he wasn't interested in debating the issue. "I'm here to see Gerald. He's taking the Owens case. Then I'm out of here."

Chris had originally intended to meet with Gerald in a few days and on a unit far, far away from Ray Owens. However, given the order from Florence to meet immediately, the best they could arrange on short notice was to get together between Gerald's meetings on Alpha unit. It was hardly ideal, but now that the case had become highly politicized, neither Chris nor Gerald was about to disregard Florence's directive.

"Well, good to see you," Alex said in a supportive tone.

"Thanks." On the closed-circuit monitor inside the nursing station, Chris could see Gerald entering Alpha unit.

"Hi, Chris." Gerald gave a warm smile and extended his hand. He had fly-away black hair and a boyishly charming face.

"Hey, Gerald. Where do you want to meet?"

"Doesn't matter to me."

"All right then, let's grab one of the interview rooms. Hey, Alex, are any of the rooms available right now?"

"Number Three is empty if you want it."

"We'll take it. Thanks."

Chris and Gerald were walking down the hallway when the door of the interview room next to Room Three opened. A staff member emerged and escorted a patient down the hallway towards them. Chris instantly recognized the patient—Ray Owens. He froze. His throat felt like it was caving in on him, and he broke into a sweat. Ray was wearing the hospital-issued green sweatpants and sweatshirt. His hair was greasy, and several days' worth of beard covered his face.

The two men made eye contact, and Chris struggled to draw a breath.

Ray flashed a smirk at Chris. "Hey, Ryder, how's your shoulder?" He suddenly lunged at Chris but was restrained by the nurse, who activated his personal security pen, triggering a piercing alarm throughout the ward and bringing several additional staff racing towards them. Ray kicked and flailed his arms while being wrestled to the floor. "Hey, Ryder, you're not out of the woods yet!" he sneered, laughing menacingly as the orderlies pulled him up from the floor and marched him off to a seclusion room while Chris stood paralyzed in a frozen stupor as the action swirled around him.

"Let's go, Chris," said Gerald. "We'll talk somewhere else." He could see that his friend was in rough shape, and he was furious. "They want us to meet so badly, we'll do it... at Manny's. I'll drive."

Chris didn't say a word as he followed his friend.

Manny's Pub was a ten-minute drive from IFP. Under normal circumstances, P.J.'s would have been Gerald's choice—closer and known for their excellent nachos. But P.J.'s was the go-to pub for IFP hospital staff, and Gerald, worried that reporters would know this, decided that the last thing he or Chris needed was to have photos of them entering a pub gracing the front page of the *Sun*. Besides, the incident on Alpha unit had made it abundantly clear to Gerald that Chris was in no shape to be interviewed anywhere near the hospital.

"How're ya doing, buddy? The beer's on me."

"Thanks, Gerald. But I'm gonna need something a little stronger. Rum and Coke. And I've got it."

"I thought beer was your thing. You planning on being here awhile?"

Chris didn't respond. He looked like his head was in a fog and Gerald wondered whether his friend was planning to get himself stone-cold drunk to keep his mind clouded. Gerald was under pressure to get information from Chris on the Owens case as soon as possible, but after witnessing what had happened on Alpha unit and looking at Chris now, he knew he wouldn't be getting this information today. He didn't care. He was more concerned about Chris' state of mind.

"That was pretty messed up back there, huh?"

"I guess," Chris mumbled. He stared at the ice cubes in his glass.

"Hey, Chris, you okay?"

"I'll be okay once I have another drink." Chris held up his empty glass and motioned to the waitress for a refill.

"No, I mean about what happened on Alpha. You kind of zoned out back there." The waitress returned with another drink for Chris.

"Yeah... well..." Chris' thoughts trailed off. A minute passed. "You know... I saw Stephanie today. Damn, she looked good."

"Stephanie Rowe?"

"That's the one. Did you know we almost went out?"

Chris took another swig of his drink, polishing it off. He motioned for the waitress, who returned with a third glass, giving Gerald a concerned look as she set it down.

"Really? When was that?"

"Years ago, before your time."

"You bullshitting me?"

"She still looks amazing. That's all I could think about when I saw her today. How much I wanted to—"

"So how did the meeting go?" Gerald was becoming uncomfortable. Chris rarely drank anything stronger than beer and he had never seen him drink like this before. He knew Chris was going through a difficult time with his separation, but hearing him go on about Stephanie while completely ignoring what had happened with Ray Owens was disturbing. He wanted to stop his friend before he said or did anything that he would later regret. Chris had helped him when he was going through troubles of his own with his partner a few years back and Gerald figured it was time to repay the favour.

"PSTD," Chris slurred suddenly.

"What? Is that what she thinks you're going through—PTSD?"

"Yeah." Chris fixed his gaze on his drink.

"So why the hell did you come back to work?"

Chris, having gulped down his drink, poured the minuscule ice cubes into his mouth. "I keep thinking about his rifle. Can't get the image out of my head."

"Hey, Chris. That's serious shit. But it's normal, you know what I mean? He tried to kill you, but you survived."

Chris ignored him. "I kept looking through the barrel. And then I had it. I had a chance."

"What? You grabbed the gun?"

"Yeah. And you know what I can't stop thinking about?"

"What, Chris?"

"I should've killed him when I had the chance."

"No, man. That's not you. You wouldn't do that."

"I wanted to. I really did." Chris' voice trailed off and he said something incoherent. A moment passed. Then, suddenly: "It's like that song."

"What song?" Gerald asked, confused.

"The Who song."

"I don't know what you're talking about, Chris."

"I won't get fooled again."

"What are you saying, Chris?" Gerald was having a hard time keeping up with his friend's drunken ramblings.

"Next time... Next time, I'm gonna blow his fuckin' brains out."

"Let's go, Chris. I'm driving you home."

# EIGHTEEN

*Saturday, February 11, 10:09 a.m.*

Elizabeth Carrier awoke from a fitful slumber. She had vowed not to fall sleep in the presence of her captors, but after countless hours of unbearable fear, her exhausted body betrayed her and she drifted off.

She didn't know why she had been kidnapped or what her captors had in store for her. Two men took turns guarding her. They did not speak to her, and she prayed they would leave her alone. But they didn't. Her face burned and angry tears came to her eyes as she recalled how one savage had taken pleasure in fondling her breast. He had slapped her face hard when she squirmed away from his fingers as they groped their way into her bra. In that moment, she had wished she were dead.

Elizabeth listened now to determine whether her abductors were in the room. With her eyes blindfolded, she couldn't tell for certain. She knew only that her body hurt from being bound with ropes to a wooden chair. She couldn't scream, as her mouth was gagged with coarse cloth. She yearned to see her mother and father, but she was terrified that she would never see anyone else ever again.

# NINETEEN

*Saturday, February 11, 10:09 a.m.*

Chris woke up on his couch, his mouth parched and head pounding, still wearing his clothes from the day before. Sunlight was shining through his window, and the television was blaring at a volume he found intolerable with his raging hangover. It struck him that it was Saturday and not—thank God for minor miracles—a scheduled workday. He was in no position to do anything but rest for the day.

He moved too quickly from his couch, lost his balance, and felt sick to his stomach. He sat down heavily, giving himself a few minutes. After an eon, he felt strong enough to stagger to the bathroom for a glass of water and three extra-strength ibuprofen. Returning to the living room, he saw his phone was blinking. He hit the playback button. Gerald had called, checking to see how he was doing. His manager rang to say he needed to talk with him as soon as possible. There was no message from Stephanie, but Chris knew he had no choice but to contact her for a follow-up appointment to discuss his confrontation with Ray Owens. He glanced at his television and caught a dust-up between a cackle of panel members on *Jerry Springer.* Hadn't the show been canceled? He realized he was avoiding calling Stephanie. He reached for his planner, located her office number, and placed his call.

He had expected to get Stephanie's voice recording, but she answered instead, explaining she was finishing an overdue report. She had heard about his recent plight and sounded empathetic and accommodating, offering an afternoon appointment. He took the appointment time, figuring it would be best to get it over and done with rather than wait for Monday. He lay his phone down and flaked out on his couch to catch more sleep. He was wasted.

Just as he was drifting off, he was awakened by a call from Deanna. "You sound groggy. Did I wake you? I thought you might be up by now."

"Yeah, I'm up. I was just resting before a meeting in a few hours." He didn't mention that his meeting was with Stephanie. For reasons that he didn't fully understand, Deanna had never warmed to Stephanie, and he wasn't in the mood for a confrontation. "What's up?"

"I was just calling to remind you about tonight? Ann Marie is looking forward to seeing you. Are you up to seeing her? Maybe just for a few hours?"

"Absolutely. What time should I come by?"

"Well..." She paused. "I'm going out tonight... so I was hoping you could come by after supper. How about six-thirty?"

*She must be going on a date.* Although curious, he knew better than to pry. "Yeah, six-thirty's fine with me." He felt alone. Deep in his heart, he knew it was for the best that he and Deanna had gone their separate ways, but that didn't prevent him from wishing for a better resolution.

"Chris, are you okay?"

"I'm fine," he said. "Just a bit tired, that's all."

"All right. See you this evening."

Chris looked at his watch. He had a few hours before his appointment with Stephanie. If he left immediately, he could get in a quick run. His head and stomach told him differently. The thought of bouncing up and down after the night he'd had made him nauseous. He opted instead for a long, hot shower and an even hotter coffee.

As Chris' taxi approached the IFP complex, he felt a pang in his stomach. He wasn't sure whether it was nerves about returning to the place where Ray Owens was being held, or his hangover. Either way, he wasn't looking forward to his meeting: Stephanie would have fresh evidence to plead her case that he was not well. He made his way to her office. This time, he wasted no time in knocking on her door and opened it slowly, "Hey, it's me."

"Hi, Chris. Make yourself comfortable. Want some coffee?" Stephanie appeared to be working on a report.

"No. I've had my fill for today, thanks." He was staring at Stephanie's ivory skin, marveling at how lovely it looked, wondering how soft it would be to touch.

"So how are you doing?" Stephanie's question abruptly brought Chris back to the moment.

*There's a loaded question if ever there was one.* "You tell me."

"I don't want to start off like this, Chris. And I don't think you really want to, either."

Chris sighed. "I guess not. What I meant was, I'm sure you heard what happened yesterday, right?"

Stephanie nodded. "David told me. He also talked with my manager. They're asking me to continue seeing you for the time being, given that it's a *unique* situation—their word, not mine."

"And David wants to hear from you before I return to work. He told you that, too?"

Again Stephanie nodded. "It's not a punishment, Chris. You came here yesterday and really pushed for an early return. Against my better judgment, I agreed. I take as much responsibility for that as you do. I think it was too early. I don't think you were ready. That's my professional opinion."

Chris looked around the office, glancing at the framed degrees on the wall along with an obscure French painting that he guessed had some type of relevance to the human condition. Finally, he replied, "It was all my fault, Stephanie. Not yours."

"So tell me, what happened?"

"I saw him—Ray Owens—and I froze."

"Was that your first indicator that something was wrong, or were there earlier signs?"

Chris realized his answer to this question would have implications for his return to work, but he opted to come clean. He took a deep breath before answering, "My sleep has been crap. I have flashbacks where I keep discovering the body—James Carrier's body. I have nightmares about Ray Owens. I get sick to my stomach just thinking about him. So yeah, there have been signs."

Stephanie nodded. "What happened when you saw Ray

Owens?"

"I didn't know what to do. I didn't do anything. I couldn't do anything. It was like I was in a dream. I just... froze. I don't know any better way of saying it. I froze."

Now it was Stephanie who took a deep breath. "Thank you, Chris. For being honest with yourself. How long have you been having the nightmares?"

"Pretty much since day one."

"Do you remember them? Are they the same each time?"

"Yeah. There was a point on the trails where he...where Ray had his rifle pressed up against my head. I was on the ground. He was standing over me, looking down with that stupid smirk on his face. And... and there was nothing I could do about it." He finished in a rush of words.

"You felt powerless?"

"Yeah, I felt powerless. I can't shake that image—that feeling. I hate him so badly. But there's nothing I can do about it. Goddamnit." He could feel his face growing hot and his muscles tensing, and fought to keep from losing control.

"You still feel powerless?"

"Yeah," he admitted in a defeated voice.

"So what happened? He obviously didn't shoot you in the head."

"I don't know... I can't remember."

"Can't remember? Or don't want to remember? Or don't want to talk about it?"

"Jesus, Stephanie. I'm trying here."

"I'm not criticizing you, Chris. I'm searching for more information. To determine whether you may have blocked out the memory, either consciously or subconsciously."

He took a deep breath and leaned back in his chair for

support. Reliving his experience from the trail was making him extremely uncomfortable. "I had pissed him off. I was trying to get inside his head, trying to distract him so that I could grab the rifle. That's when it happened."

"What happened?"

"He hit me across the face with the rifle and then pressed it against my forehead."

"Then what?" Stephanie leaned forward.

Chris' skin was becoming clammy, his breathing quickening as anxiety bubbled inside of him. He tried to focus on the question. "I kept pushing his buttons. I knew it was working, so I kept it up and seized the chance when it came. He took a swing at me and missed. And I grabbed the gun."

"And you're alive today because of your actions."

"Yeah," he whispered. "I guess I am."

"You discovered Ray's weakness. You exposed it, and capitalized on it."

Chris nodded and relaxed a bit in his chair. He could feel the wetness of his shirt, but his breathing was returning to normal.

"Because you helped the police, he was apprehended. A killer is off the streets because of you." She paused to let that sink in for Chris before going further. "It seems to me that far from being powerless, you actually took control of the situation."

Chris knew what Stephanie was doing. She was reframing his trauma, highlighting the positive aspects of his actions and the positive outcome. This was a technique he could have predicted—he used it himself with his patients. To his surprise, however, it was working for him now. He felt a huge sense of relief that he had finally taken what was percolating inside his head and brought it out into the open. "I guess you have a point."

There was a lull in the conversation. Stephanie broke the silence. "I think we've made great progress here today. What do you think?"

"Yeah, I agree." Chris felt physically and emotionally drained, but for the first time in days, he also felt hopeful about his future.

"We should probably stop for today and set another appointment."

Chris was perplexed. "Look, Stephanie, I can do that, but it may be hard to find the time. In between work and Ann Marie, you know. How many more appointments are you thinking?"

"It's difficult to nail down precisely how many may be necessary. And I don't want to rush this. We've already seen what happens when we rush through this process."

"Yeah, but I really need to get back to work. I mean, I was counting on going back as soon as possible."

"I'm sorry, Chris, but I don't think you're ready to return yet."

"Well, what the hell was this all about today? A waste of time?"

"Absolutely not. You've made great gains here today. But it isn't as simple as one breakthrough session and that's it—case closed, problem solved. The brain doesn't respond to trauma that way."

"What am I supposed to do in the meantime?" He felt himself getting anxious. He was uncomfortable with having his position as a social worker reversed, and finding himself in the role of patient.

"That's a good question. Why do you feel so compelled to return to work so soon? Is your identity wrapped entirely around your work? Is that healthy? Those are questions for you to think about, Chris." Stephanie put her pen down. "This is a time for you to restore a healthy balance to your life. Making the most of your time off work can be very healthy for you... and your family. To—"

"What's my family have to do with this?"

"That's another question I think you should ask yourself."

"Goddamnit, stop answering every question with a question. Look, I have to go back to work. I really do."

"Why? Tell me why that's so important to you?"

He paused. *Why* was *it so important?* "Each day... that I'm not there... I feel like he's winning. That Ray's winning. I need to go back... to show him that he hasn't won." He caught himself off guard with this revelation.

"Chris, why are you so preoccupied with Ray Owens, besides the obvious fact that he tried to kill you?"

He hesitated. "You're going to think this is messed up, and it probably is."

"Go on." Stephanie leaned forward.

"I feel like I know him. Like I've run into earlier versions of him all my life." He paused. "When I was a kid, there was this bully Wayne. My aunt called him 'Wayne the Pain.' He'd march into the neighbourhood looking for trouble. For some reason he always singled me out."

Chris hadn't thought of Wayne in years, but just uttering his name brought him back to those painful days of his youth. *"Gimme your Doritos, Ryder." "Gimme a spin on your new bike. Oops, didn't see the curb. Guess it's not new anymore." "Gonna run home crying to your mommy? Oops, I forgot, you don't have a mommy."* Chris' bubbling anger brought him back to the present.

"It wasn't just that he beat the shit out of me when I didn't do what he said. Or that he made a fool out of me in front of my friends." He took in a breath. "What really hurt was how he made me feel about myself. I started to hate myself." He could feel his emotions slipping out of control and stopped momentarily, avoiding eye contact with Stephanie, before continuing. "After a while, I began to hate the feeling of hating myself. I didn't want to feel that way anymore. I'd rather have my nose bloodied than to cower and feel that way. My Aunt Mary knew something was wrong. She took me to see someone. She also bought me weights and signed me up at a gym where I started running and started getting stronger. I swore that I'd never *ever* back down to Wayne again. And I didn't."

Chris looked at Stephanie, who remained speechless. "I despise people like Ray, the way he treats other people, the fact that he thinks the rules don't apply to him. But as much as I despise him, I know him. Just like he gets inside my head, I think I can get inside his." He fell silent.

Stephanie spoke softly. "Thank you, Chris, for sharing that part of your life with me."

"So now you know why I have to go back to work and show Ray that he hasn't won."

"I do understand where you are coming from, Chris. But explain to me how this is *healthy* and why I should be persuaded to go against my better judgment a second time in supporting your return to work?"

"I think he's playing a game. I think he planned on coming back to IFP for a reason—to play with me."

"If that is indeed what he is doing, the stakes are too high to be playing his game."

"I know that. Believe me, I really do. But...you've heard about the missing woman—Elizabeth Carrier?"

"Yes?" Stephanie gave Chris a puzzled look.

"She's the daughter of one of Ray's victims from Woodland Park. The police believe Ray may be connected to her disappearance."

Stephanie looked confused. "Okay, but what does this have to do with you?"

"I think he's a sick, twisted psychopath. I think he wants to use me in some sort of game involving Elizabeth Carrier."

"Even if that were true, look at the risks involved. How would that be fair to you?"

"It's got nothing to do with fair. Whether I like it or not, I have to play along with him... if it could help *her*."

Stephanie paused, reflecting on what she had heard. When she spoke again, it was in a low voice, as if she knew it would elicit an angry response from Chris. "You need to know... that Ray Owens... is not Stan Edwards."

"Jesus, Stephanie. Where the hell is that coming from?"

"I think you know what I'm saying. I know about Stan Edwards."

"Dammit, Stephanie! You're bringing up stuff that I told you a long time ago. Stuff from the past, from *our* past. All that shit belongs back there. You have no right to bring that up now."

"No, it needs to be said, Chris. Because I think the man who murdered your mother when you were a boy still haunts you. But Ray Owens, as bad as he is, is not Stan Edwards. And saving Elizabeth Carrier will not bring Fiona back."

Chris threw his hands in the air. "You're absolutely... I can't believe what I'm hearing! Do you actually believe what you're saying?" He could feel his blood running hot. He looked away from Stephanie, desperately trying to regain composure. "I feel so... betrayed. I told you about my mother because I trusted you. I told you serious, personal stuff back then—stuff that didn't come easy for me. And now you're using it against me. That's just—"

"Sorry, Chris. That wasn't my intention. I want to help you. I'm worried you're on a very dangerous path. I see patterns between how you struggled over what happened to your mother and what you are going through now. If you don't deal with the parallels you have created between Stan and Ray, it will continue to haunt you. You could get yourself killed. Ray Owens is a monster."

"Wow. Is that your deep psychological diagnosis for him? He's a *monster?* Is that the best you can come up with?"

"Chris—"

"You're really something else, you know?" He shook his head.

"Listen to me," Stephanie said passionately. "You left yesterday, upset with what I had to say. But look what happened when you went back to work. I don't want you to get hurt."

Chris had heard enough from Stephanie. He stood up, shoved his chair back against the wall, and stormed to the door, ready to leave. "What the hell does it matter to you what happens to me?"

"Because I care about you. I... I have feelings for you."

"You... what?"

"The truth is... well, I still have feelings for you." She

fiddled with her pen as she began to blush. "I thought I had buried them, but seeing you again made me realize they're still there." She took a deep breath. "So you see, I know a thing or two about living with the past too. I know I need to be honest with myself and with you about my feelings. And I could tell from our meeting yesterday that you still have feelings for me. I—"

"Jesus, I..." Chris felt a confusing mixture of emotions and wasn't sure what had affected him more—Stephanie's comment about his mother, or her confession about having feelings for him.

"I'm sorry, Chris. The last thing I want to do is hurt you—like before."

"Some things are better left in the past. That's what I've told myself all these years. When there's nothing you can do about it."

"But sooner or later, Chris, the past catches up with you. You have to deal with it, one way or another."

"Not today. I have to go, Stephanie. I've got to pick my daughter up." He walked out the door, utterly bewildered.

Driving to Deanna's house to meet Ann Marie, Chris replayed his conversation with Stephanie. His life was unraveling, and he wasn't sure how to put it back together. He thought about canceling his outing with Ann Marie, but realized she needed stability and predictability in her life. And he needed the stability that his daughter provided as well. He'd called ahead to ask Deanna to hold off on Ann Marie's supper, as he hoped they could go out for a meal together. Pulling up in front of the house, Chris could see his daughter looking out the window. She raced past the front door and jumped into her father's arms, and he enveloped her with a big hug.

"Hey, sweetie. Do you feel like Wilbur's tonight?"

"But Daddy, we go there for breakfast."

"Who says we can't have breakfast for supper?" He tickled her side.

"You're silly," Ann Marie laughed.

Deanna walked down the stairs, wearing a dress Chris couldn't remember seeing before. "Wow, someone's going out tonight!" He resisted the urge to pry for more information.

Ignoring his comment, Deanna simply stated, "I shouldn't be any later than ten. Is that okay?"

"Sure." Chris felt awkward and knew better than to press any further.

Deanna leaned down to give Ann Marie a kiss on her forehead. "Don't forget to brush your teeth before bed, okay? I'll check on you when I get home."

"Okay, Mommy," Ann Marie replied, oblivious to the awkwardness between her parents.

Deanna glanced at Chris. "Have a good night."

"You too." He turned to Ann Marie and whispered, "Are you ready to have a good night, just you and me?"

"Yes, Daddy," she said with a big smile.

"All right then. Wilbur's, here we come."

On the drive to the restaurant, Ann Marie filled her father in on the details of her day.

Wilbur's was the epitome of a greasy spoon, but was a local favourite for its hearty breakfasts and friendly staff. Ann Marie cheerfully ordered waffles with strawberries while her father went with his usual scrambled eggs and toast. Ann

Marie was busy mushing her strawberries in whipped cream when Chris felt compelled to tell his daughter, "You know I love you, right?"

"Of course, Daddy." She kept her eyes on her waffle.

"And you know I will always love you?"

Ann Marie looked at her father and gave him a funny look. "Daddy, you're silly."

Chris marveled at her sapphire blue eyes and silky brown hair. "I know I'm silly. But I want you to know that I love you. Mommy and Daddy both love you very, very much."

"I know." Ann Marie picked up a strawberry with her fingers and playfully dipped it into an extra thick layer of whipped cream. Chris silently watched her, finally satisfied that the drama between her mother and him was not having an obvious adverse affect on her.

After eating, he offered Ann Marie the choice of bowling or a movie at home. She deliberated for a few seconds before deciding on a movie. When they got home, she ran to her bedroom to change into her pajamas. She returned with her *Princess Ariana* DVD and an accompanying princess doll that Chris assumed was Ariana. Ann Marie took great effort to pose her doll in a precise sitting arrangement as she cuddled up to her father.

As Ann Marie blissfully talked along with the movie's dialogue and gave her father a commentary on every scene in the movie, Chris watched her with a mixture of amazement and melancholy. She was the picture of innocence and joy, and he wanted to capture this moment and frame it forever in his memory. He wanted Ann Marie to retain these beautiful characteristics of wonderment and happiness even as he hoped to shield her from a world of cruelty and sorrow. He feared this fleeting moment of tranquility would soon give way to an uncertain future, but he was more determined than ever to protect his daughter from the Ray Owenses of the world.

# TWENTY

*Sunday, February 12, 3:33 p.m.*
*Our Father who art in heaven, hallowed be thy name. Thy*
*Kingdom come...*

Elizabeth Carrier lost count of how many times she had said the Lord's Prayer. She hadn't been particularly religious up to this point in her young life. But now that she was clearly in her moment of need, she reached out to a higher power.

Sensing that her captors had temporarily left her alone in the cabin, she exerted every ounce of strength she had left in an attempt to wiggle her hands free from the rope that bound her to a hard wooden chair. She felt the skin on her wrists being rubbed raw against the coarse rope, and she realized her wrists were now bleeding. She cried out in pain and in desperation for someone to save her, but fearing that her time on this earth was coming to an end. *Our Father who art in Heaven, hallowed be thy name. Thy Kingdom come...*

# TWENTY-ONE

*Monday, February 13, 8:03 a.m.*

Ray lay on his bed. He was glad to be out of the seclusion room, but seeing the helpless look on Ryder's face had made it worth it. Now he was mulling over the mind games he would play with that bitch-shrink Stevenson—he'd been eagerly waiting for this chance ever since his admission to the hospital. *Beat the mindfuckers at their own game.* He knew the manipulation routine better than anyone and relished the thrill of schooling the fools. They were so pathetically easy to take in. His scam was to feign symptoms of mental illness during his admission at IFP and trick everyone into believing he was out of his mind when he committed his crimes. In court, he would represent himself, at which time he would launch a defence strategy arguing that he was now cured from his symptoms of mental illness. He would then seek an absolute discharge from all criminal charges. He had rejected the services of a legal aid lawyer. *What the fuck do they know?* Ray intended his day in court to make a mockery of the mental health and justice system, and the very thought aroused him.

Alex, the head nurse, appeared at Ray's door and advised him that Dr. Stevenson was ready for him in the interview room. *She's ready for me? What a joke. I'll go when I'm damn well ready,* and he purposely stalled his arrival at the meeting, saying he had to make a bathroom stop. While there, he pissed all over the floor and plugged a toilet. *That'll teach them to mess with me. S*atisfied that he'd kept the psychiatrist waiting long enough, he emerged from the bathroom and let Alex escort him to the interview room.

Ray entered the cramped room and took a seat. He recognized Dr. Stevenson. The shrink introduced him to another moron, some social worker named Gerald Reed. *I guess Ryder's skipping this party. What a pity.* Ray smiled widely and extended his arm to shake their hands, starting with the shrink. *Showtime.*

"Dr. Stevenson, it is a pleasure to see you again. I'm hopeful you can help me through this difficult period."

Dr. Stevenson stole a glance at her colleagues as she shook Ray's hand. "Thank you, Mr. Owens."

"Please, call me Ray. May I call you Marilyn?"

"I'd prefer you call me Dr. Stevenson."

"Very well, Doctor, you're the boss." Ray smiled. The shrink started rambling on about the non-confidential nature of their interview and the purpose of the assessment. Ray, bored out of his mind, managed not to yawn in her face, and interjected, "Marilyn... forgive my transgression... *Dr. Stevenson*, I will cooperate with you to the fullest as I have complete faith in your abilities to help me overcome my affliction."

"What affliction are you referring to, Ray?"

*Bingo.* "Oh, Dr. Stevenson, I continue to be tortured by the most horrendous of voices. You will remember we talked about this when I was last here, and that I had come to believe I was possessed by the devil himself. I only wish I'd been able to receive the necessary help by medical professionals such as yourself in keeping the devil at bay. But he has returned." He paused for effect. "The other voice, I fear, is that of the unfortunate crippled soul I... I had the misfortune of coming into contact with three years ago."

"You're referring to Mr. Dobbin, the man who died as a result of the injuries sustained from your offence?"

"Yes, sadly. Not a day goes by that I don't grieve the loss of this poor man. They say there are no victimless crimes, and I must agree. For I have come to see that he, as well as I, became the tragic victims of my most horrific disease." *Ha! The fuckers are falling for my story—hook, line, and sinker.* But when Ray glanced at the social worker, he appeared to be glaring back at him. *What's this asshole's problem? You'd think I'd pissed in his Corn Flakes.* Then he realized the moron was probably upset over what had happened to Ryder. He also wasn't sure what the shrink was thinking.

"Well, Ray, we'll discuss the voices you say you hear in a little while. But for now, I need to ensure that you are fully aware of why you are here. You have been charged with a number of criminal offences. Do you know what they are?"

Ray gave Dr. Stevenson a friendly smile, while inside he was enraged with her. *How dare that bitch try to control this interview?*

*She'll learn. She'll definitely learn.* Ray dramatically clutched his forehead in mock discomfort. "Oh. The voices are unhappy with me for talking with you. I need to return to my room to rest my troubled mind. May I leave?" He looked at the shrink, knowing she had no choice but to let him leave.

"Yes, Ray. I'll come see you tomorrow."

"That would be so good of you. What time were you thinking?"

"It doesn't matter what time. The staff will come and get you. And Ray, just a reminder that another outburst like the one you had on Friday with Mr. Ryder and you'll spend the rest of your admission in seclusion. Thank you. You can go now."

*She can't dismiss me like that,* he raged to himself. Ray felt his blood burning but fought to ensure he maintained a pleasant facade. "In that case, I will pray that I feel better tomorrow. Thank you so much for your time, *Marilyn*."

Alex, Gerald, and Dr. Stevenson looked at each other before Alex rose to his feet to escort Ray to his room. On Alex's return, they debriefed their meeting at length. They were unanimous in their opinion that they had witnessed a desperate attempt by Ray to control the interview.

"I don't know what his game is yet, but it's clear that he's playing some type of game with us all," Dr. Stevenson said.

Alex nodded in agreement. "We've observed no evidence of psychotic thinking or disorganized behavior from Ray while he's been on Alpha unit."

"We'll need to remain vigilant," Dr. Stevenson concluded. "Document each and every interaction and observation with Mr. Owens. We'll need this to support my position in court. Unfortunately, I believe he's just getting started."

# TWENTY-TWO

*Monday, February 13, 8:03 a.m.*

Bone-weary after yet another sleepless night, Chris groped for the television remote by his side. His new routine involved waking in the early hours of the morning and switching on the television. He would scan multiple useless channels until finally throwing down the remote in exhaustion. He would then close his eyes for another couple of hours as the cycle repeated itself.

He knew work was not an option until he had the go-ahead from his manager, who would consult with Stephanie. Yes, he could ask his union to bring a grievance against the process, but he wasn't interested in bringing any more attention to himself with his employer. And he was trying hard to block Stephanie from his mind, but she kept creeping back.

He turned his thoughts to Sergeant Ryan and realized he was avoiding him as well. The very notion of returning to Woodland Park to retrieve the missing cell phone made him tense up. His shoulder twitched, reminding him of the wounds he'd suffered on the trail. Then he remembered the words Ray had uttered with his contemptuous smirk—*You're not out of the woods yet*—and he was filled with a renewed motivation to return to the park, to prove that he would not live in fear of Ray Owens. *I will survive this.*

Chris pulled his truck into the Woodland parking lot and stepped out into the grey, overcast day. As he walked toward the trail, he tried to ignore his pounding heart and clammy skin. *Stephanie would say I'm engaging in exposure therapy— returning to the trail, the source of my trauma, to face my fears.* Smiling grimly, he realized that Stephanie was once again occupying his thoughts, but he was too tired to block her out.

Their last meeting had left him debating a number of issues in his head. He knew Stephanie was right to be concerned about his symptoms of PTSD. He wondered if she was also right with her comments about his mother's death, a painful chapter in his life he had always desperately attempted to ignore. Above all, he was still trying to make sense of the bombshell she had dropped about her feelings for him. He had always felt there was a part of Stephanie that remained a mystery to him, and now he was once again intrigued with her.

From the first time he'd laid eyes on her close to ten years earlier, Chris had been strongly attracted to Stephanie. She was blessed with a natural beauty, and he'd spent many an aching moment contemplating what it would be like to explore every inch of her body. Even during his last two meetings with Stephanie, he found himself captivated by less obvious features of her body—the way her eyes crinkled when she smiled, the way she twirled her luxuriant hair around her finger. Seeing her again, talking with her again, reminded him how much he missed the sound of her voice.

But the attraction was not solely physical. Chris felt at ease around Stephanie in a way he did not with anyone else. They shared a natural compatibility. *Maybe the timing is finally right for us*, he thought, and just like that, he was walking with a spring in his step.

His thoughts about Stephanie were a welcome distraction as he walked along the trail. He was even beginning to feel good about his decision to return to the park—until he realized he was approaching the path he had taken when Ray attacked him. His stomach knotted, his chest tightened, and he felt like he was going to pass out. *Oh, Jesus, is this what a heart attack feels like?* Rationally, Chris knew it was nothing more than an anxiety attack, but he could do nothing about it as he relived his fight with Ray over the rifle and felt the icy barrel of the rifle pressed into his forehead. Too dizzy to walk, he slumped to the ground and closed his eyes, waiting for the moment to pass. He finally summoned enough energy to ignore his shaking body and lifted himself unsteadily onto his feet. Forging further into the park for the cell phone was no longer an option; he could not bear the thought of stepping another foot on the trail. The only thing he could do was retreat back to his truck in defeat. *Stephanie is right. This isn't over.*

Back at his apartment, Chris called Stephanie to book an appointment. She sounded unusually restrained, but had an opening later that afternoon. He was quick to grab it.

That gave him several hours to kill. He was feeling antsy and not sure what to do to fill the time. He took his iPod from its dock and chose a selection of Pearl Jam songs, and "In Hiding" rang through his apartment. After a hot shower, he paid extra attention to picking out his clothes. He grinned as it dawned on him that he wanted to look his best for Stephanie.

On his way to her office, Chris thought over what he would say to her. He would have to tell her about his agonizing experience at Woodland Park and acknowledge that she was right. He would start the meeting on a positive note and see where things led them from there. Aware of his nervousness *and* excitement, he knocked on Stephanie's door.

"Come in, Chris."

Stephanie looked tired, and from her tone, Chris sensed that something was on her mind. "Is everything okay?"

"I don't think so."

"What's wrong?"

Stephanie paused. "I thought a lot about what you said during our last meeting. You were right about a few things."

"I said a bunch of stuff, and some of it was because... because I was pissed off. But I'm over that now."

Stephanie took a deep breath. "I blurred the line between our professional and personal relationship. You made a comment about feeling betrayed. And.. .and I think you're right. I shouldn't have done that." She looked visibly uncomfortable and avoided making eye contact.

"Well, I said some things too. I mean, that's what I wanted to say to you today. You made some good points last time that really made me think."

"But I let my personal feelings get in the way of my work

with you."

"I don't know, Stephanie. Part of me thinks that it's because of our past that you were able to help me see things... more clearly."

"I appreciate what you're doing, I do. But..." She paused, struggling with what to say next. "The truth is, I knew about your separation. When I heard about the opening at IFP for contract work, I took it—with you in mind. I wanted to see you. I shouldn't have assigned myself to your case. That was a mistake. I think it's best that I refer you to someone at EAP, who can follow through with you. I think that—"

"Come on, Stephanie. We've been through that. Is it really necessary?"

"I think it is. It's clear to me that you're going through a very difficult time and someone at EAP will be able to help you."

"That wasn't what I meant..." Now it was Chris who struggled for the right words. "I thought we were getting somewhere. I mean, I was getting somewhere from our meetings. Can't we just continue?"

More silence from Stephanie. "Are we going to pretend I didn't say what I said last time? I can't. My personal feelings are clouding my professional judgment. I can't do that."

Chris felt deflated. This was not going the way he had hoped. And yet he knew Stephanie was right. He couldn't ask her to continue with something that she thought was in breach of her professional practice standards. "Whatever you think is best. I'll obviously go along with it."

Stephanie breathed a sigh of relief. "Thank you, Chris, for being so understanding. I believe it's for the best."

*I've heard that before.* Chris thought back to what Deanna

had said to him six months earlier when they had separated. "What will you say... you know... about the reason for the recommendation to EAP?"

"I've thought about that. And I haven't found a good explanation—except the truth."

"So you're going to tell them you want to sleep with me?" Chris joked.

Stephanie blushed. "Well, I wasn't exactly going to put it that way."

"I'm sorry. I don't mean to make light of what you're saying."

"It'll be okay. The fact is, you were originally referred to me as part of critical-incident debriefing, which was designed for support, not treatment. It'll be my recommendation that an appointment with EAP is warranted, and it's likely your manager will strongly encourage you to attend an initial meeting."

Chris debated how he should ask his next question. Finally, he just blurted it out: "Are you going to be saying anything about my mother?"

"Would that bother you if I did?"

"It's just that it... complicates things. Makes larger issues out of things than they need to be."

"How so?" Before he had a chance to respond, Stephanie added, "First of all, the content of our meetings remains confidential. And I wasn't planning on mentioning your mother, but I'm curious why you asked."

"Because my manager doesn't need to know about my past—that's none of his business. But... but I'm not a fool, Stephanie, and I know you're not either. I shared stuff about my mother before and... well, when I try to look at things from your perspective, I can see why you might see a connection. Between her and Stan Edwards and Ray Owens and me."

"Chris, I don't think it's a coincidence that your mother and you both chose helping professions—nursing and social work. You are empathetic with your patients, and from what I hear, you are very compassionate towards their families. I believe the difficult experiences you had growing up with your own family makes you attuned to the struggles you observe with your patients' families." She paused. "I know your mother died when you were young."

"She didn't die, Stephanie. She was killed. There's a difference."

"I'm sorry, Chris, I didn't mean—"

"No, it's me who's sorry. The truth is, that night when I was on the trail... when Ray..." Chris breathed deeply. "When he held the rifle on me, I actually thought about my mother. I thought, this is how she must have felt when Stan Edwards took her hostage in that hospital. For some messed-up reason, I thought about her." He bowed his head and massaged his temple, looking away from Stephanie. "Jesus. What am I doing, talking about this?"

"Go on, Chris. Don't stop."

"Then I thought of how he had killed her. And more than anything, I didn't want to give Ray the satisfaction of killing me. I didn't want to let him win. You were right. Ray did remind me of Stan. But..." He stared off into the distance, not knowing what to say next.

"Chris, I won't be mentioning your mother. But that doesn't change my concern about your preoccupation with Ray Owens. It's not healthy, and—"

"I know. I know it's risky for me to play his game.

Believe me, I would love to walk away from this and never hear his name again. But, like I said before, I really don't have a choice."

Stephanie remained silent. Chris felt the need to change the topic—quickly. "So where do we go from here?"

"Well, I'll send my recommendation to your manager. I should have it done by tomorrow."

"That's not what I meant. What about... *us*?"

Stephanie fidgeted in her chair. "What do you mean?"

Now it was Chris' turn to blush. "From the moment I saw you, I haven't been able to get you off my mind."

Stephanie was silent for a minute. "I don't want to complicate things any more than they already are, Chris."

"My marriage is over. Believe me, it's over and has been for longer than I care to admit." He sighed. "It's for the better. Deanna's dating."

"I'm sorry to hear that."

He shrugged. "It is what it is. But I feel like... well, maybe you and I have a chance here." He paused, took a deep breath. "So how about it? Will you take a chance on me?" Chris laughed nervously as he thought of the song with the same title. "If it will help, I'll even sing that Abba song for you. What do you say?"

Stephanie smiled despite herself, but then said in a serious tone, "I don't know, Chris. I just don't know. I think we need to go slow and see where things lead."

"What about supper? Tonight. I can pick you up."

"I'd like to, but I'd feel a whole lot better if we waited, at least until we are no longer officially working together."

"What, you can't be seen in public with your clients?" He had meant it as a joke, but once the words were spoken, he realized his comment was touched with sarcasm. "Sorry about that. That didn't come out the way I meant."

"I know what you meant."

"You'll give me a call then, or let me call you?"

"Yes. I'd like to. It would be nice to get together."

"All right then. I'll wait." He extended his hand to her. What he really wanted to do was to place his arms around her but knew he couldn't. The way he was thinking about her, he was unlikely to stop at a friendly hug. So they shook hands. Chris detected a slight blush in Stephanie's cheeks.

Chris decided to check in on his colleagues in the social work department. Lately he'd been a stranger to their normally tight-knit group. Working in a dynamic setting with constantly shifting demands and challenges meant they had to trust and rely upon one another. He had always been proud to be a part of this team. He found Gerald on the phone in his office and waited until his friend had hung up before announcing his arrival.

"Hey, Chris, good to see you, man."

"Good to see you too."

"Take a seat. How are you doing? The last time—"

"Yeah, I'm sorry about the other night. I got a bit out of hand."

"That's not what I meant. I know... Look, we all know it's a brutal time right now for you. Is there anything I can do to help?"

"No, I plan to be back to work soon. I hope you haven't had to cover too much for me. You know, in addition to the

Owens case."

Gerald shook his head. "Man, that Owens is something else." He proceeded to fill Chris in on Dr. Stevenson's interview with Ray as well as his own brief interactions with the man. "The guy's a psychopath. The staff on Alpha can't wait to get rid of him. He's stirring the shit pretty bad there, instigating fights between patients and trying to get them fighting against staff. You name it and you'll find Owens in the thick of it."

Chris shook his head. "Yeah, he's bad news." He needed to change the topic. "So how's everybody else in the department doing?"

"Good. I mean, it's busy. It's always busy; what else is new? We're hanging in there. We'll be glad to see you back, that is, when you're feeling up to it."

"Yeah, hopefully soon. I've been seeing Stephanie... uh, professionally, that is." He felt his cheeks burning as he remembered how he'd drunkenly talked to Gerald about Stephanie a few days earlier.

Gerald brushed off his colleague's awkwardness. "You know, Chris, the more I think about it, I can really see you guys together." And then with an attempt to elicit a smile from Chris, he added, "You make such a cute couple."

Chris' face turned red. "We'll have to see about that. Well, I guess I'll let you get back to work."

He headed to his own office, aware that he needed his manager's clearance before returning to work and was taking a risk in disobeying David's directive, something he would never do under normal circumstances. *But these are not normal circumstances, and I have to do what I think is right.*

He spent the next few hours returning phone calls to his

patients' families. For many patients, as in the case of Paul Butler, this was the first time their loved one was in trouble with the law. For many patients, it was also the first contact with mental health services, let alone the Institute of Forensic Psychiatry, so family members were full of questions, filled with sadness, shock, guilt, and confusion. Chris found working with patients' families to be challenging but also among the most rewarding aspects of his job.

He had first spoken with Paul's mother Susan a few weeks earlier after Paul's admission to IFP. Her world had been turned upside down by her twenty-two-year-old son's erratic behaviour, which had culminated in criminal charges. Susan had tearfully told Chris that her son had been complaining for several weeks that he was receiving disturbing messages from his television and computer. In an effort to prevent evil spirits from entering the family home, Paul had closed all the blinds in the house and blocked the heating vents.

Susan had explained how she'd tried to seek help for her son, who had become too scared and suspicious to even venture outside the house. He had misunderstood her efforts to help him and was becoming increasingly paranoid. In the midst of an intense argument, Paul had thrown his computer out his window and rampaged through the home, threatening his mother. Susan had wept as she described how the police came and advised her to have charges laid against her son, as a way to ensure he received the help he needed. As a result, Paul had been ordered to IFP for a psychiatric assessment.

In a subsequent phone call, Susan had revealed that her son had first been diagnosed with schizophrenia about two years earlier. Until recently, he had been taking his medications and never been violent or in trouble with the law.

Chris' telephone call with Paul's mother today lasted over an hour. He could tell that she was guilt-ridden about calling the police, and she expressed anxiety about whether her son's mental health would improve. He answered her questions on Alpha unit and the court process.

He also updated her on Paul's progress at IFP. At the end of their conversation, Susan told Chris she hoped to visit her son the following week. Although she lived several hours away, she wanted to make the visit as his birthday was approaching. Chris took down the details and said he would make special arrangements with the staff on Alpha unit to permit flexibility when she arrived.

Although he was exhausted by the time he left his office at the end of the day, Chris welcomed the opportunity to focus on his patients instead of thinking only about Ray Owens and the fate of Elizabeth Carrier.

# TWENTY-THREE

*Tuesday, February 14, 2:07 a.m.*

Elizabeth's captor was bored from being cooped up in the cabin and decided to pass the time by having fun with her. "Hey Princess, wake up, it's Valentine's Day." He laughed at the sight of the girl being jarred from her sleep as he uncovered her blindfold. "You got a special someone in your life? Yeah, I bet you do. I'll bet you're a real fuckin' tease." He sized her up for the umpteenth time, fantasizing about the hot slender body wrapped underneath her clothes. His eyes locked on hers and she quickly looked away. "What's your problem? I'm not good enough for you? You wouldn't fuck me if I was the last guy in the world?" He laughed heartily. "Believe me babe, I just may be the last guy you ever see in this world."

He saw the look of terror on her face. "Hey, just saying. Don't blame me, I'm just doing my job, that's all. If you want someone to blame, blame your fuckin' father. None of us would be here if it weren't for him. But he was taken care of, too."

Now tears were streaming down the girl's face and he

realized that she hadn't figured it out. "Oh, damn, hate to be the one to break it to ya, babe. But, yeah, your old man is dead. Sorry," he said sheepishly. "But don't worry, it won't be much longer, you'll be joining him. Now get some sleep. You look tired."

# TWENTY-FOUR

*Tuesday, February 14, 2:07 a.m.*

Ray lay wide awake on his bed, his mind churning. It was late, but he rarely slept through the night. He wasn't thrilled to be confined in this shithole. *I'm surrounded by retards and goofs.* And being grilled by the head shrink. *She's lucky she doesn't see me alone; I'd rip the bitch apart.*

He reminded himself once again that being here was a necessary step in exacting revenge against Chris Ryder. He held Ryder partially responsible for his prison sentence three years ago. And it was Ryder who had found his cell phone, which threatened to place his freedom in jeopardy again. But he—little Ray Owens—had big plans for Ryder. News that would rock Ryder's world and make his life a living hell. And *that,* Ray had decided, was worth risking his freedom.

Besides, he was making the most of his situation. Pitting patients against staff and against each other was becoming an amusing way to pass the time. He'd already started other patients complaining about the poor quality of meals on the unit. And he'd managed to get others demanding more time off the unit to enjoy fresh air and exercise. He laughed aloud at how the suckers were falling for it—hook, line, and sinker.

Ray smiled even more broadly as he replayed his latest encounter with Ryder a few days earlier. *The fucker froze like a deer in the headlights.* Ray felt a rush as he thought of the plan he had in store for Chris Ryder in the coming days. *You ain't seen nothing yet.* He snickered as he broke into the song of the same name. He was aware that his loud singing was disturbing the other patients from their sleep, so he sang even louder.

# TWENTY-FIVE

*Tuesday, February 14, 10:00 a.m.*

Chris opened the door to his office, set his bag down, and logged onto his computer. At that day's early-morning meeting with an EAP counselor, he wasn't surprised that most of their session had revolved around a discussion of PTSD, and he had reluctantly consented to a series of follow-up appointments. He'd even agreed when the counselor had advised him to take his time with his return to work, and Chris had made a point of saying all the right things about pacing himself and taking it day by day. Less than five minutes after leaving the EAP office, he was on the phone with his manager, confirming his schedule for the next day. Nor, he decided, had he any intention of following through with subsequent appointments. *Some things I just have to deal with on my own. Always have, always will.*

He had hoped to spend the morning navigating through the pile of emails that were staring back at him. But word had spread that he was back, and his plans were interrupted by colleague after colleague stopping by to see him. Some gave a gentle pat on his shoulder, while others expressed sympathetic words of encouragement. There were even some, he figured, who had dropped by just to see what kind of state he was in. He made sure that he said all the right things—that he was happy to be back, that he was taking it day by day, that he was putting it all behind him.

In truth, he had a plan, and Ray Owens factored prominently in it. He knew Ray was playing a game with him, and it irked him that Ray had won the last round. Chris wanted to return to Alpha unit to show Ray that he was back. He had no intention of saying or doing anything to Ray, but figured his very presence on the unit would send a strong message. The problem was that his friends and colleagues were too solicitous. Every time one of them dropped by his office to wish him well, Chris cursed underneath his smile because he was being delayed in accomplishing his goal.

Finally by late morning, he was ready to venture down to Alpha unit, where he had arranged to meet Gerald to go over the Owens case. Gerald had strongly urged a different setting, but Chris insisted on meeting on Alpha, explaining that this was an important part of his ongoing rehabilitation— an argument that, he realized after he voiced it, was actually true. He was still feeling anxious about the prospect of seeing Ray, but knew he had to face his fears. Going to the remand unit would be an important step in that direction.

His mouth was dry and his heart raced as he approached Alpha unit, but he did his best to let the anxiety pass through him. Using his fob key to gain entry to the ward, he checked in at the nursing station. It was buzzing with activity.

Alex was the first to greet him: "Hey, look who's back."

"Good to see you too."

The nursing station was crowded with two psychiatrists, a family practitioner, and a throng of nurses, all of whom looked over at Chris. He suspected they were wondering if he would fare any better today than he had the last time he'd set foot on the ward. "Is Gerald around?"

"Yeah," said Alex, "he's in the interview room right now. Should be done soon."

Chris checked his watch. In less than two minutes, patients would be leaving their rooms and gathering in the main dining area for coffee. He was counting on seeing Ray, so he waited patiently. On cue, a health-care worker announced that it was coffee time, and the door to the dining area opened and patients started filing into the room.

Paul Butler timidly approached Chris and said in a mild voice, "Can I talk with you for a second?"

"Sure, Paul. What's up?"

"My mother is visiting me this weekend. The staff told me I should talk with you about her visiting outside of regular visiting times. I think she's going to call you."

"That's been taken care of. Your mother and I spoke about it earlier, and I've cleared it with the unit. I hear you have a birthday coming up. I hope it's a good one."

"Thanks." Paul smiled broadly.

The sight of Ray swaggering into the room interrupted Chris' conversation with Paul. They locked eyes, and Chris was reminded of how much he loathed Ray's smirk. He knew that the nurses were keeping a watchful eye on them both, but he wasn't planning on causing a scene. On the contrary, he didn't want to show any reaction to Ray at all, so instead he casually walked to the nursing station to wait for Gerald, who arrived a few minutes later.

As he left the dining area with Gerald, Chris glimpsed Ray out of the corner of his eye. "You're not out of the woods yet, Ryder!" Ray shouted, but Chris refused to engage him. Ray continued to rant as Chris walked away, wondering what the hell he was rambling about.

After his meeting with Gerald about the Owens case, Chris dropped by his manager's office to discuss his work schedule, then spent the remainder of his day following up on casework that had accumulated while he was away. In the late afternoon, he checked in briefly with Dr. Stevenson to catch up on their patients, including Paul Butler.

"Paul's doing very well with the change in his medications," Dr. Stevenson said, "and he's fully cooperating with the court assessment. The nursing staff report that he's been a model patient on the unit."

"I spoke with him earlier about his mother's visit. You should have seen his face light up when he started talking about his birthday. It made my day." As they talked, Chris realized he was once again working with Dr. Stevenson as part of a team and was finally settling back into a routine.

Driving away from the building later that afternoon, Chris was tired but content with how his day had progressed. Turning on the car radio, he caught the end of a news item about the lack of leads in the investigation into the disappearance of Elizabeth Carrier. His mood turned somber as he thought of the pain that the family would be enduring, grieving the loss of one member while frantically searching for another. He turned off the radio to distract him from these gloomy thoughts and instead focused on Stephanie and the plans they had made for that night.

Stephanie, her resistance finally worn down, had agreed to get together with Chris that evening. However, she asked that they take things slow and suggested somewhere neutral, like a restaurant. Chris made reservations at Marcello's and insisted on picking her up at her condominium.

He had every intention of taking things slow that evening— until he saw Stephanie at her door in a red dress that perfectly accentuated her body. She smiled at Chris. His breathing became laboured and he lost his ability to concentrate on anything other than wanting her. And he knew that Stephanie knew. She muttered an unconvincing "We shouldn't, Chris" and, for an instant, they remained frozen, looking at each other in anticipation of the next move. Then Chris closed the door behind them and pulled Stephanie's body against his. He whispered, "You're so beautiful," as he kissed her lips, caressed her neck, and ran his fingers through her flowing hair. Stephanie's eyes remained closed, and her breathing became heavier as Chris ran his fingers along her back, searching for the opening to her dress. Locating the zipper, he pulled the dress from her body. As it fell to the ground, he lowered Stephanie to the floor and continued kissing her lips and neck, making his way to her breast. Wanting her so badly that he fumbled at unbuckling his belt, he kicked off his jeans, bracing his body atop Stephanie's.

"No, Chris. We can't... I can't..."

"Come on, Stephanie. You can't be serious?"

"Oh God, I'm sorry. It's just too soon. I want to... just not yet. Not tonight."

"Then when? Jesus." He looked away in frustration as he

lay on his back next to her, his breathing slowly returning to normal.

"Sorry, Chris."

"Well, put some clothes on, for God's sake. You're torturing me here."

"I can see that," Stephanie said sheepishly, sneaking a last look at Chris' naked body as he put on his jeans. He watched her as she slipped her dress over her head. Now dressed, they lay together on her floor, silently looking up at the ceiling.

"Well, I guess we could order in," he said with disappointment in his voice.

"I'm sorry, Chris. It's just that I told myself I wasn't going to let this happen. Not tonight."

He tried to lighten the mood. "You shouldn't have worn that damn dress—on Valentine's Day, of all days."

"I didn't mean to lead you on."

"I know. I didn't intend for this to happen either. But I'd be lying if I said I regretted trying."

"It's just that... well... this complicates things."

"Life is complicated, Stephanie. After the past few days, I also appreciate that it's fleeting. We've got to make the most of these moments."

"My, aren't you the philosopher?" She playfully poked his arm. "Well, we have to eat something. You're right, maybe we should order in. Then you're going home."

"Yeah, I figured as much. I feel so used." He sighed dramatically. He stood up, aware that Stephanie was checking him out. He felt flattered until he realized she was looking at the latest scar on his shoulder. Tears were forming in her eyes, and Chris enveloped her with a warm embrace. "That's over now."

Stephanie wiped her eyes. "I hope so, Chris."

# TWENTY-SIX

*Tuesday, February 14, 10:10 p.m.*

Ray had stalked Alpha unit, looking for his latest prey. It hadn't taken long to choose his victim—Paul Butler. That fucker Ryder had had the audacity today to ignore him, choosing instead to talk with the boy. Never mind, he told himself. Paul would do just fine. He had all the qualities he looked for in a victim: he was innocent, naive, and most important of all, unaware.

Ray pretended to befriend Paul. He'd even come to the younger man's defence this afternoon when another patient, Steven, had accused Paul of going into his room and taking his money. Naturally, it been Ray who had stolen the money— and it was also Ray who had told Steven he'd seen Paul enter his room. All Paul knew, however, was that Ray had stepped in when big bad Steven was about to pulverize him, so in Paul's mind, Ray had become his protector, a person he could trust.

Ray laughed. He had plans in mind for poor innocent little Paulie. Big plans.

# TWENTY-SEVEN

*Tuesday, February 14, 10:10 p.m.*

As he drove back to his apartment, Chris tried to make sense of what had happened that evening with Stephanie. A week ago, he could never have imagined her back in his life. But then again, he could never have imagined the return of Ray Owens either. Between Stephanie, Ray, Deanna, Ann Marie, Elizabeth, and work, Chris could feel his life becoming increasingly complicated. He turned on his radio in time to hear U2's "Beautiful Day." Hearing it now brought Chris renewed hope about making Stephanie part of his life, and he sang along to the song.

He thought of his daughter. He had agreed with Deanna's request to switch his usual day with Ann Marie, but now realized he missed her. He would call her when he got home. His watch told him she would be asleep, and he wasn't sure that he was prepared for a conversation with her mother right now. There was just too much going on, and he wouldn't know where to start or what to say.

At home, Chris looked around his empty apartment. He had never liked it because it felt sterile, devoid of life. He knew he hated it simply because he didn't share it with anyone, and it had reminded him of how lost and lonely he was. The apartment had represented the end of an important part of his life. Every time he walked through the door, he was confronted yet again by this reality.

But tonight, he saw something different. He saw potential—a new beginning. He smiled as he remembered Stephanie's comment about his newfound philosophical insight. Then he chuckled, basking in the glow of *almost* getting laid.

Whatever the source for his new outlook on life, Chris finally felt ready to move on. For the first time in a week, he slept through the night.

# TWENTY-EIGHT

*Wednesday, February 15, 9:04 a.m.*

Chris arrived at his office re-energized and ready to take on the day. Going through his voicemail, he found a message from Sergeant Ryan asking to discuss the Owens case. Although he wanted to put as much distance as he could between himself and Ray Owens, he felt obligated to return the call.

The sergeant sounded relieved to be hearing back from Chris and proceeded to update him on the James Carrier case. When he was done, Chris asked, "Have there been any developments in locating Elizabeth Carrier?"

"Unfortunately, no. That's why I was calling you. To see if Owens has mentioned anything about her."

"Not that I'm aware of." Chris paused before adding, "And even if he had, I wouldn't necessarily know because I'm not involved in his case." He told him about his director's order to stay away from Ray Owens.

"That's too bad, Chris. I figured you'd have the best shot at getting information from Owens."

Feeling a combination of guilt and frustration building up, Chris shot back, "He damn near killed me, Brandon. Besides, I'm not a police officer. We both know there are limits to what I can do."

"I know that, Chris," Brandon said. "You have your orders, and I have mine. Technically, I shouldn't even be talking with you right now. But let's face it, neither of us is particularly conventional in how we do our job."

"What makes you say that?"

"You made a choice out there on that trail. You could have kept running. But you didn't. And I believe you're interested in helping find Elizabeth. It's also pretty obvious to me you want Owens brought to justice. We're alike in that way. I've read Owens' police file. We both know what he's about. He's killed before, and given the chance, he'll kill again. You said yourself that he's playing games with you guys." He sighed. "Look, I've been around long enough to know that sometimes it's hard to find the justice in the justice system. The courts are backlogged, and as much as it pains me to say it, there's corruption in the system. But I think we both share a desire to prevent him from slipping through the cracks—again."

"What can *I* do?"

"Off the record, Chris, we stand a better chance of bringing down Owens if you and I pool our resources and share information with each other."

Chris felt familiar troubles washing over him. He desperately wanted to cut his ties with Ray. In fact, he wanted nothing further to do with the bastard. But Brandon was right—Chris knew he would never be able to live with himself if he didn't do everything within his power to help Elizabeth Carrier. "So we both think Ray is behind Elizabeth's

THE KILLER TRAIL D.B. CAREW

disappearance?"

"I think he knows something about this case that he's not telling us."

"I don't get why he would have taken her. And how."

"At this point, there are a variety of possibilities. For all we know, he could have lured her to him after her father's murder at Woodland Park. So far, all we know about James Carrier is that he worked as a freelance journalist. His widow is too devastated to talk to us right now. We're respecting her wishes and giving her time to grieve. Carrier didn't have a criminal record and, according to his brother, no known enemies either. The reality is, Owens may be the only person who can lead us to Elizabeth. All I'm asking is to keep your ears open around him. It's our best chance—maybe Elizabeth's only chance. Let's talk again, soon."

*What the hell are you planning, Ray?* Chris slammed the phone down on its cradle.

Chris returned to his phone messages. Paul Butler's mother had a number of questions about her upcoming visit with her son. He called her back and addressed her concerns. He knew that patients at IFP (and, by extension, their families) often faced the double stigma of having a mental illness *and* a forensic label as a result of their contact with the legal system, and he valued his role in his team's efforts to break down those negative stereotypes.

With twenty minutes to go before rounds, Chris decided to hunt down some fresh coffee. Coffee was part of his daily routine—as were his never-ending promises to provide the supply *the next time*. The ritual also gave him a perfect opportunity to check in with his colleagues and catch up on the latest hospital gossip. Today's topic was Natalie's birthday lunch at P.J.'s. Chris had been invited to come along, but had politely declined, citing the mountain of work waiting for him on his desk, although the real reason was that he knew he would be asked about his ordeal at Woodland Park and he wasn't feeling up to discussing it yet.

At Alpha unit, Paul Butler approached Chris. He looked anxious. Chris figured he was simply worried about his mother's pending visit, so he was surprised when Paul placed a note in his hand and hurried off without saying a word. Opening the envelope, Chris read a single scribbled line: *You're not out of the woods yet, Ryder.*

*Ray Owens.* He was stunned. Why was Ray was using Paul as his messenger?

"Hey, Paul, wait up." Paul stopped. Chris caught up to him. "What's with the note, Paul?"

"Uh, what do you mean?" He looked uncomfortable.

"You just gave me a note. Why?"

"I... I don't know."

"What do you mean, you don't know?" Paul's face was flushed and he was talking nervously. Chris didn't want to escalate the situation, but he was becoming increasingly uneasy. He started over. "Paul, you handed me an envelope." He produced the note and presented it to him. "Did Ray Owens ask you to give this to me?"

Paul appeared too scared to answer and instead left the room with his head hung low. Chris was furious that Ray was using Paul to do his dirty work. He raced into the nursing station, spotted Dr. Stevenson, and waved the note at her.

"We've got a serious problem here!"

"What's this about?" She read the note.

"It's from Ray."

"Did Ray give this to you?"

"No. But I'm pretty sure he gave it to Paul, who gave it to me."

"Did Paul confirm that Ray gave the note to him?"

Chris shook his head. "No. Paul wouldn't say. But come on, who else would do this?"

"Chris, this doesn't mean anything. At worst, it looks like a senseless prank. Nothing more." She handed the note back to him.

"Damnit. Don't you see what he's doing? He's using Paul to get to me. We've got to get Paul off this unit before Ray does something to him."

Dr. Stevenson motioned to Chris to follow her into the medication room for privacy. Once inside, she gave him a stern look before stating bluntly, "Paul is going nowhere." Then, in a softer tone, "Chris, you've got to pull yourself together. I know the last several days have been difficult for you. And I know it's hard for you seeing Ray Owens in here."

"Jesus. It's more than that, Marilyn—"

"No, it's not. Listen to me, as your friend. I'm working on getting Ray out of here as fast as I can. In the meantime, reduce the amount of time you spend on this unit. Does—"

"Yes, yes. But what about the note?"

"What about it? Look, you have no evidence it's even from Ray to begin with. And even if it is, it's clear that his intent is to taunt you. And it's working. Look at yourself. Listen to yourself. You've become preoccupied with him. He's making a fool out of you, and you're not helping things."

"What the hell does that mean?"

"People are talking. Your last incident with Ray. Stephanie Rowe."

"What about Stephanie?"

"Oh, for Pete's sake. You know nothing remains a secret in this place. It's become public knowledge that you two are seeing each other." Marilyn took a deep breath before continuing. "Look, I know you've been going through a difficult time with your separation from Deanna and with everything that's happened in the last little while. But dating at work? At this time? As your friend, I've got to say, it hardly shows good judgment on your part."

Chris ignored the comment. "Marilyn, you don't understand. Ray is a master manipulator."

"Oh, I absolutely agree with you in that regard. And it's *you* who is being manipulated. Now, enough about Ray Owens."

From the intense way that she placed her hands on her hips and stared at him, he knew that it would be in his best interest to change the topic, but he was unable to let it go. "How is your assessment on Ray going?"

"Chris, did you bloody well hear *anything* I just said? I am *not* going to discuss this case with you. That's the end of it." She stormed out of the medication room.

*Am I the only one who sees what's going on?* Chris asked himself as he left the medication room.

By the time Chris said his goodbyes and left the nursing station, the patients were all in the dining area for coffee. He searched for Ray and found him staring back with a sneer on his face.

"Hey, Ryder, did you get my note?" he shouted from across the room.

The other patients immediately stopped what they were doing, sensing an imminent showdown. Alex, the head nurse, motioned to his staff inside the nursing station to come out as reinforcements to subdue the situation before it boiled over.

Chris felt his face burning, and every fibre of his body wanted to charge at Ray, to pound his fists into the man and wipe the smirk off his face. But there was a risk of other people getting injured in the fracas, so he gritted his teeth and took a deep breath. With a forced calmness, he said, "I don't know what you're talking about. You must be confused."

Ray frowned. "Oh, okay, Ryder. Maybe I'll give Paul another message for you. And," he added with a snarl, "there'll be no confusion next time."

Chris' composure abandoned him completely, and he charged towards Ray in a rage. Alex intercepted him while a burly health-care worker blocked Ray's path. "You leave him alone, you hear me!" Chris yelled at Ray, who was grinning widely in delight. Alex ordered Ray to his room; Ray complied, but not before aiming a twisted smile at Chris.

Alex ushered Chris back into the nursing station. "What the hell was all that about?"

Chris was still simmering with anger. "Goddamn, I hate him."

"Look, you've got to get it together. You can't be pulling shit like this."

Chris took a deep breath. "I'm sorry, Alex. I guess I messed up there, didn't I?"

"Damn right. That was not cool." Seeing the tension still on Chris' face, Alex added in a calmer voice, "You keep acting like this, they're going to end up banning you from this unit or even suspending you. You know that, right?"

"Yeah, I know," Chris said defeatedly. He made his way out of the nursing station and off the unit, pissed off that he had just lost another round to Ray.

On his way home, Chris called Deanna to see if he could drop by to take Ann Marie out for supper. It was not his scheduled day with his daughter, but he thought he'd give it a try. He felt as if somehow he was slipping out of her life, and he could certainly use some of her cheerful chitchat after the day he'd had.

He had called Stephanie earlier that afternoon, but she had told him she was busy for the evening, working on an overdue report. She hadn't sounded like herself, and Chris wondered if she was putting off seeing him after the awkwardness of their previous evening. In any case, he'd decided he wouldn't force the issue. Instead, he hoped for a pleasant evening with Ann Marie. Deanna answered the phone on its third ring.

"Hi, Dee. How are you?"

"I'm okay. Is everything okay with you? You sound tired."

"I'll be all right. I was wondering if it would be okay if I came by to see Ann this evening."

"I'm sorry, Chris. She's having a play date at her friend's house. She won't be home until sometime after supper."

"Oh. Well, it was worth a try. I don't suppose you're free tonight?" He was feeling desperately lonely but instantly regretted his question. *I sound so pathetic.*

There was a pause. "Actually, Chris, I'm not alone. I... have someone over."

Shit. It suddenly dawned on him that he was interrupting Deanna's own play date. He felt foolish for calling.

"Ah... okay... well... give Ann a hug for me." *All the women in my life are turning me down.* Chris realized he was going to be spending the evening alone after all. *Just Captain Morgan and me.*

# TWENTY-NINE

*Thursday, February 16, 2:54 a.m.*

Pretending to be asleep, Ray surreptitiously watched Neil, the night nurse, complete his three o'clock rounds. He found it laughable how easy it was to trick the idiot into believing he was sleeping when in fact, he was awake and fully aware of his surroundings. Ray had quickly figured out the routine and knew exactly when Neil did his nighttime flashlight checks on patients to ensure they were breathing and accounted for in their rooms. Neil would now go back to the nursing station until the next check at four o'clock.

The coast clear, Ray stealthily emerged from his room and crept down the dark hallway to Paul Butler's room. Paul was sleeping soundly, and Ray was hard-pressed to withhold a laugh at how easy his offensive was turning out to be.

"Sleep tight, sucker," he muttered as he approached his target. Cramming a sock in Paul's mouth, he delivered a flurry of vicious blows with fists and elbows to Paul's head, leaving him a bloody mess. Ray turned the younger man over onto his stomach, covering him with his blanket.

The hallway was as deserted as before as Ray calmly crept back to his room, thinking defiantly, *You won't miss this message, Ryder. Don't fucking ignore me.*

# THIRTY

*Thursday, February 16, 9:11 a.m.*

When Chris arrived at work the next morning, he found his manager waiting in his office. Had he overlooked a nine o'clock meeting? He couldn't recall one on his schedule, which meant David's impromptu visit must be related to yesterday's run-in with Ray. Chris couldn't remember exactly how much Captain Morgan he'd had the night before, but he foggily figured he might have had about three glasses too many.

"You look like hell, Chris," David said.

"Just a bit of a late night, that's all. Nothing that a strong cup of coffee can't help." David looked unconvinced. "Sorry I'm a bit late. Is everything okay?"

"You tell me, Chris."

"Like I said, I didn't sleep well last night. But I'm okay."

"I heard what happened, Chris."

"Nothing much happened. And it's over with now, anyway."

"No, I don't think it is over. I'm assuming you haven't

heard about Paul Butler."

"Huh? What happened to Paul?"

"He was taken to Health Sciences Centre early this morning. It appears he was attacked in his room at some point during the night. Night staff—"

"Oh my God, is he okay?" Chris could feel his pulse racing.

"We don't know yet. The doctors think he has a concussion, among other injuries."

"Jesus! Do we know..." Chris was halfway through his question when he realized he knew the answer. "It was Ray, wasn't it?"

"We don't know that Ray was involved in this altercation, Chris. We'll be passing what information we have on to the police. And we'll be doing our own internal review. But—"

"Goddamnit! Did any of the staff see anything? What about the other patients?" Chris' anger was rapidly rising.

"Staff saw nothing. As for the other patients, either they really didn't see anything or they're afraid of repercussions if they talk with staff. We—"

"Jesus!" Chris slammed his fist on the desk. He suddenly thought of the closed circuit video monitors installed on the unit. "What about the cameras, did they pick anything up?"

David sighed. "The picture quality is grainy given that the main lights were off at that time of night. And Ray, uh, whoever did this made a point of covering his head with a towel and avoided looking at the camera. It's clear he knew what he was doing and manipulated our schedule for night checks."

"That's Ray! It's got to be. Shit!"

"I know how you feel. The truth is, you're not the only

one who thinks Ray is behind this. But we need proof, so please be patient and let the investigators do their job."

"Are you kidding me? We already know who did this!"

David spoke in a quiet, measured tone. "Listen, Chris. You're an excellent social worker and well respected in this hospital, and I personally enjoy working with you. But the events over the last several days have been traumatizing for you and it's showing in your behaviour. You should go home and make a follow up appointment to see your worker at EAP. We can—"

"Did anybody call Paul's mother? Does she know? I've got to tell her."

"Chris, listen to me!" David shouted. "You are not calling his mother. We'll handle it. I'll have Gerald do it. You're in no state to be calling anyone right now. I want you to go home and get some rest."

"I can't do that, David. There's—"

"I'm not asking you, Chris. As your manager, I'm telling you. Do you hear me?"

"David—"

"Do you hear me?"

"No. I don't hear you. I can't believe what I am hearing. This is bullshit. You don't—"

"Chris, I'm going to stop you right now before you say anything else that you'll end up regretting. I'm giving you twenty minutes to clear up the rest of your day. Then I want you to leave. And I will check with Security to confirm that you've left. Is that clear?"

Chris took a deep breath and weighed his options. He wanted to visit Paul in the hospital but knew he'd need authorization from his manager. "David, can I say something?"

His voice was calm but tight.

"What is it, Chris?" David's voice was also substantially more composed.

"I admit the last little while has been tough. And I know I've made some mistakes. But I'm not out of control. I know what I'm doing. I'm just asking for another chance. Will you give me one more chance?"

"What are you asking me, Chris?"

"Let me visit Paul at HSC. I feel awful about what happened to him. I just want to check in on him. And I want to make the call to his mother."

David paused to consider the request. A critical-incident review was being ordered into the attack, so the therapeutic rapport Chris had developed with Paul and his mother might prove useful for damage control if the Butler family lodged a complaint against IFP for the incident. Moreover, the social work department would come across favourably for maintaining contact with the Butler family.

"All right. You can visit Paul. We have one of our security officers stationed outside his room. I'll let him know you'll be dropping by. And, yes, you can call his mother. But then I want you to go home for the remainder of the day. Is that clear?"

"Absolutely," said a relieved Chris.

"Promise me you'll stay away from Ray Owens." David wasn't looking forward to doing damage control with his superior, Florence Threader. He'd have to explain how Chris and Ray continued to have confrontations with each other despite orders from Florence that they remain separated.

"I'll stay away."

The Health Sciences Centre was a forty-minute drive from IFP. Along the way, Chris stopped at a Starbucks. As he waited for his venti-sized coffee, he glanced through the day's *Sun*. It was the same old same old. The Canucks had lost their third straight game. There had been another targeted hit on a gang member by a known rival fighting for control over the drug trade. Some politician was going on about fighting the scourge of organized crime in the city; Chris didn't know much about this Charles Longville but passed him off as just another politico using crime to further his own agenda.

He flipped through the pages of the newspaper until he saw the headline, "Still Missing: Elizabeth Carrier." The police were remaining tight-lipped about the investigation into her disappearance and were asking members of the public to come forward with any information. He flashed back to the gruesome image of James Carrier's body at Woodland Park. He couldn't begin to imagine how the Carrier family must be coping with the added pain of a missing daughter.

Chris was sure Ray had played a role in the disappearance of Elizabeth Carrier just as he was sure Ray had been responsible for the assault on Paul Butler. *It was Ray who was the real scourge on society*, Chris thought to himself. His mind went once again to a dark place that was becoming frightfully familiar—a world rid of Ray Owens, a world where he, Chris Ryder, had come up with ways to make Ray disappear. *What the hell is wrong with me?* Horrified, he shook the morbid fantasy from his mind, started his truck, and headed toward Vancouver to visit Paul Butler.

The majestic snow-capped North Shore Mountains gleamed in the distance as Chris entered the city. In a perfect world, he'd be heading to Cypress Mountain for a carefree day of skiing or kayaking in Deep Cove or mountain biking on Burnaby Mountain. But this was not a perfect world, and Vancouver itself—home to both wealth and poverty, beauty and decay—was the epitome of contrasts and contradictions. One minute, Chris would find himself in the maze of the notorious Downtown Eastside, driving past a homeless man pushing a shopping cart filled with his worldly possessions through an alley littered with used syringes. In the next instant, he would be driving through Gastown with its high-end retail stores and restaurants. He passed a car with a British Columbia license plate boasting "The Best Place on Earth." *I guess it depends on where you're looking.*

At the HSC, Chris introduced himself at Reception and was told Paul Butler was on Six North, the Intensive Care Unit. Taking the elevator up to the ward, he tried unsuccessfully to shake the memories of his own recent admission to the hospital just days before.

He recognized the IFP security officer standing outside Paul's room, following standard procedure for patients attending appointments outside the confines of the Institute.

"Hey Horace, how's it going?"

Horace looked pleased to see a familiar face. "They told me you were coming."

Chris nodded. "David got me clearance with your department and the ICU. I wanted to check on Paul. How's he doing?"

"He hasn't moved much the whole time I've been here. The doc checked on him about thirty minutes ago."

"Okay if I go in?"

"Be my guest."

Chris took a deep breath to prepare himself. He wasn't sure what to expect, but he'd seen enough evidence of Ray's violence in recent days to know firsthand the brutality that humans inflict upon each other. Shame for having harboured similar thoughts about harming Ray overwhelmed him. *What am I becoming?*

The walls of the room were coloured pea green, and the all-encompassing smell of disinfectant made Chris' stomach queasy. Paul was hooked up to a myriad of tubes and blinking and beeping machines, adding to the discomfort Chris felt whenever he visited such places. Paul's eyes were swollen shut, a bandage wrapped around his forehead. Chris could see spots of red where blood had seeped through the dressing.

Paul was sleeping. Chris felt helpless standing over him, but he knew he had to visit. *I'm responsible for his injuries. Paul became Ray's target because he'd seen me talking with him.* He walked over to Paul's bed and leaned in towards him. He could hear Paul's laboured breathing. "Shit, Paul, I'm so sorry," he whispered, knowing that he couldn't hear him or even know that he was there. Then his sadness gave way to anger and he added, "I'm going to make him pay, Paul. I promise."

He tiptoed out of the room and engaged in some idle chitchat with Horace about the Canucks before leaving the ICU. His heart heavy, he thought about the difficult conversation that he was about to have with Paul's mother.

After an emotional phone call with Susan Butler, Chris left the HSC and returned to his truck to begin the drive home. But he found himself instead being drawn to Kitsilano Beach and the Pacific Ocean sparkling in the early afternoon sun. He walked along the beach, letting the cool breeze blowing in from the ocean wash away some of his sorrow and anger, eventually settling on a park bench that provided a panoramic view of mountains on the horizon and the high-rise buildings of downtown Vancouver in the foreground. He was hypnotized by the rhythmic swaying of sailboats while seagulls squabbled with each other in the clear blue sky. He watched a young family playing on the sand in the distance, throwing a tennis ball to their black Labrador retriever.

Closing his eyes and listening to the waves crashing against the rocks, he slipped into a state of tranquility and began wondering what his life would be like if he were to board one of the boats and set sail for new land.

He was jerked back to reality by the screeching of sirens responding to a crisis somewhere in Vancouver, reminding Chris once again of the contrasts and contradictions of his beloved city.

At home, Chris had barely enough energy to kick off his shoes before collapsing, physically and emotionally exhausted, onto his bed. He awoke disoriented and hungry. It was dark, and his watch told him it was nine o'clock. Too hungry and groggy to prepare a proper meal, he scrounged around his fridge looking for any edible leftovers. Three pieces of pizza had been sitting there for about a week. *That's all right. Everything goes down with a drink—or two.*

Checking his answering machine, there was a message from Stephanie asking if he was available to get together on Friday. "Yes!" he shouted triumphantly, only to immediately feel guilty as he thought of Paul Butler lying broken in his hospital bed and Elizabeth Carrier missing, her fate unknown. He decided he didn't have the energy to engage in a meaningful conversation with anyone, even Stephanie, in his present state, so he elected to channel surf while he drank himself into oblivion.

# THIRTY-ONE

*Friday, February 17, 3:09 a.m.*

Ray lay on his bed staring at his ceiling and plotting his next move. It was three o'clock in the morning, and as usual, he was not sleeping. *Not that any of these fools would notice,* he thought with a snarl. His assault on Paul had almost been too easy—certainly not a challenge worthy of him—but he'd accomplished what he'd set out to do and would take that as success. Still, he would've loved to have seen the look on Ryder's face when he heard the news about the attack on Paul.

Ray had picked up a few nuggets of information over the last few days. He'd read a newspaper article about Elizabeth Carrier and laughed aloud when he read how the police were checking out possible leads into her disappearance. *Ha! They don't have a clue what's going on.*

But what had really aroused Ray's attention was the conversation he'd overheard between two nurses talking about Chris Ryder's new flame, Stephanie Rowe. He'd seen her on the unit although they had not met... yet.

Ray moved his hand down between his legs and started masturbating to the image of Stephanie. It wasn't her beautiful body that made him hard, but rather the image of inflicting pain on her in front of a powerless Chris Ryder.

*I'm going to reach out and touch someone special.* And he laughed himself to sleep.

# THIRTY-TWO

*Friday, February 17, 8:09 a.m.*

After a fitful sleep, Chris woke with a raging headache and resolved to cut back on his alcohol intake. He popped a couple of ibuprofen, grabbed a hot shower, and dressed for work.

Settled into his office, he started plowing through his emails, trying in vain to ignore his feelings of nausea and lethargy. He was about to return a phone call when Dr. Stevenson appeared at his doorway.

"Have you got a minute, Chris?" She looked somber.

"Sure, come in. Something the matter?"

Dr. Stevenson closed the door behind her and sat down. "I came by to say I'm sorry. I should have listened to your concerns about Paul. I—"

"Marilyn, look, I thought Ray was using Paul, but obviously I didn't know for sure. Nobody knew what he was going to do. I feel awful, too."

"But if I'd listened to you and moved Paul off the unit, this wouldn't have happened."

"I know what you're saying. But Ray would simply have moved on to somebody else."

Dr. Stevenson sighed deeply. "One of the things I value about our working relationship is that together we see the whole picture. But I was so concerned about what was going on with you that I didn't give you the benefit of the doubt that you could be right about Ray and Paul. I also knew Ray was playing some sort of game, but I didn't listen to your warning. I'm sorry."

Chris felt a mixture of guilt and anger starting to surface, something he wasn't ready to deal with at the moment. He deflected the topic. "Has there been any update on Paul's condition?"

"No. He's still at HSC. But when he comes back, I'll make sure he won't be on the same unit as Ray."

Chris paused. "How about the assessment on Ray?"

Dr. Stevenson smiled. "No change in my opinion from the last time I saw him here. I've seen no evidence of an acute mental illness, despite his attempts to feign symptoms. He's—"

"He's faking a mental illness?"

"He has talked about hearing voices, but when pressed, it's evident to me that he's making it up. I've asked Psychology to—"

"Not Stephanie?" Chris asked, panic in his voice.

"No, not Stephanie. As I started to say, we've asked Psychology to assess him for malingering. Rory went to see him, but so far, Ray has come up with all kinds of excuses to delay testing."

"I don't want Owens anywhere near Stephanie." He blushed as the impact of what he had said set in. He hadn't meant to come across so obviously protective of her.

Dr. Stevenson graciously overlooked his outburst. "Rory hopes to administer the Psychopathy Checklist. I'm confident Ray has dominant traits of psychopathy, but I want the testing to corroborate my assessment."

"I can't remember the last time we conducted the PCL-R on one of our patients. Then again, it doesn't surprise me at all with Ray."

"You're right. In my report to court, I'll explain that the correlation between a severe and persistent mental illness such as schizophrenia and psychopathy is not strong, which is why we don't routinely include the PCL-R in our assessments. However, in Ray's case, while I don't believe he has a severe and persistent mental illness, I do believe he has prominent traits of antisocial and narcissistic personality disorder, and I will clearly emphasize that in my report. We'll see what Rory comes up with in his testing."

"If he can get access to Ray." Chris paused and took a deep breath. "From what I went through in Woodland Park, Ray is the freaking poster child for psychopathy, right down to his total lack of empathy or remorse. I doubt he'll ever agree to any type of formal assessment."

Dr. Stevenson nodded. "You're probably right. He also refuses to have a lawyer. Crown asked me about this, and I told them that I believe Ray's decision to represent himself in court is not based on any issues of mental capacity but solely on his arrogance and disdain for the system. I told you the Crown prosecutor is considering dangerous offender status with Ray, didn't I?"

"You mentioned it. I've never gone through that process. Have you?"

"Not while I've been here, but back when I worked at

West Coast Corrections."

"So how exactly will that work?"

"If Ray is convicted on his charges, the Crown will seek an indeterminate prison sentence. They'll argue that he is too dangerous to be released back into society because of his violent tendencies."

*He's too dangerous to live anywhere.* Chris reflected on the carnage Ray left in his wake. The thought depressed him and left him speechless.

Dr. Stevenson seemed to pick up on his silence. "So how are you holding up?"

Chris found he no longer had the energy to deny the obvious, or to deflect his friend's concern for him. "The truth? I'm tired."

"You look tired. Why don't you—"

"No, I mean tired of everything. Hell, I'm even tired of being tired." He shrugged.

"I'm worried about you, Chris. You've gone through a traumatic event—"

He cut her off, smiling slightly because he knew what she was going to say. "Yeah, I know, and now I have PTSD. I keep hearing about this."

"Your sessions with Stephanie. So how about it? Do you think there might be any validity to what two very intelligent women are saying to you?" She smiled.

"What I'm beginning to think is that there's a shelf life for this kind of work, and maybe I'm past my due date."

"You're not thinking about leaving, are you?" The smile dropped from her face.

"I don't know. I couldn't leave now, though, not until this whole business with Ray is over."

Marilyn looked confused. "Why? You're not assigned to Ray. I don't understand."

"I know how this is going to come across. But... well, like you said, I think Ray is playing a game. And for some twisted reason, I factor into it."

"But you don't have to play along with his game."

"I think I do. I was pretty sure he was using Paul to get to me, and unfortunately I was right. And I think—no, I'm almost positive he's connected with Elizabeth Carrier's disappearance."

"But Chris, even if he *is* connected, what are the odds that he'd tell you anything. Or even that she's still alive."

"I know, Marilyn. I've had this conversation with Stephanie, too. In the end, I'd never be able to live with myself if it turned out I could have saved Elizabeth. Ray knows this, and that's why he's toying with me. I have no choice."

Marilyn gave him a worried look. "Chris, be careful. He wouldn't think twice about coming after you."

"I know." *I'm counting on it.*

# THIRTY-THREE

*Friday, February 17, 9:33 a.m.*

C.L. walked into his office, closed the door, and placed a call to his trusted henchman Pierce Hennessy.

Hennessy picked up. "Yeah?"

"What have you got for me?" C.L. asked, an impatient edge to his voice.

"Sir, we've been searching Woodland Park, but we haven't had any luck in finding the cell phone."

"Well, what are you doing standing there?" C.L. snapped. "Don't leave that bloody park until you've ripped it apart and have that phone in your hands."

"I'll make sure we do that, sir, but I'm beginning to think it's not here."

C.L.'s face hardened. "I'm not paying you to think. I'm paying you to do what I say. Is that clear?"

"Yes, sir, it's clear."

Just thinking about the cell phone made C.L.'s face hot with anger. He'd considered the possibility that the phone was in the possession of the police, but his inside sources at the RCMP confirmed they didn't have it. That left only a few possibilities remaining, and he weighed the options available to him for retrieving it.

"I want your men to stay at the park. Maybe I'll get lucky and one of your goons will stumble upon the phone." C.L. paused. "Do whatever you have to do. Just find out whether Ray Owens or Chris Ryder has it."

"I can take them both out if you want," Hennessy boasted, eager to please his boss.

Careful not to be heard outside his office, C.L. responded in a low but cold voice, "I don't care what you do to them as long as that phone ends up in my hands. And soon." He hung up.

C.L. looked admiringly at the reflection in his mirror. He adjusted his crimson tie before getting on with his busy day. *Knock 'em dead.*

# THIRTY-FOUR

*Friday, February 17, 10:30 a.m.*

Chris closed his door behind Marilyn and returned a call to Sergeant Ryan, who was now leading the investigation into the assault on Paul Butler.

"Ray is behind this, Brandon. I know he is!" he said with disgust.

"I don't doubt you. The problem is, we need proof. None of the patients are willing to talk with us about it. Either because no one observed anything, or—"

"I know," Chris said in a tired, I've-heard-it-all-before voice. "Patients won't talk out of fear of being labeled a rat for reporting on a fellow patient. Or else they're scared shitless of Ray."

"Well, whatever the reason, we have very little to go on right now. And we haven't been able to interview Paul yet."

"Ray used Paul as bait to get to me. I'm just as responsible for Paul's beating. That's what pisses me off." He ran through his recent confrontations with Ray, including Ray's continued use of the bizarre phrase: *You're not out of the woods yet.* "Hell, he even used that phrase in the letter he gave Paul to deliver to me."

"Pretty resourceful, isn't he?"

"Resourceful, nothing. He's diabolical—that's what he is."

"And I thought my job was tough. Tell me something, Chris, why do you do this kind of work, with psychos like Owens trying to avoid jail by pretending to be insane? Aren't all your patients trying to do the same thing? It just makes me a bit weary of the whole insanity plea."

"I do it, Brandon, because I believe in the work. The greatest majority of patients I work with are not trying to fake anything—they're legitimately mentally ill. And it's rewarding to see how well they do with a bit of help." He paused, sensing that Brandon was still skeptical. "But you're right. Ray is one of those rare few trying to make a joke of the mental health system. Unfortunately, it's the Rays of the world that the general public reacts against, thinking that most patients are like him. The shame is that the forensic system works! The assessment weeds out those fakers like Ray who are trying to manipulate the courts. But if the public loses faith in the system... it's... it's like what you said about finding the justice in the justice system, people will assume it's all corrupt. And if that happens, it leads to... chaos."

The sergeant reflected for a moment before responding, "Not if we have anything to say about it, right, buddy?"

"We've got to try. I guess that's the best we can do and maybe it's enough to stop Ray."

"So what's the status with his assessment? Anything you can share with me?"

Chris told him about the psychiatric assessment being conducted by Dr. Stevenson, as well as the referral to Psychology for testing for psychopathy.

"So what kind of things are on this Psychopathy Checklist?"

"There are twenty items, including manipulation, lack of remorse, callousness, failure to accept responsibility, poor behavioural control. We believe Ray will rate high along several of them. We also think he'll be a high risk for recidivism with small likelihood for rehabilitation."

"Which pretty much means he can't be helped, right?"

"That's a hot issue right now. Unlike people with mental illnesses who respond well to medication and other forms of treatment, the research isn't clear when it comes to the usefulness of treatment for psychopaths. Programs like group therapy are offered, with the aim of helping psychopathic individuals gain insight and awareness into human vulnerability. Problem is, many of them choose instead to manipulate their new skills to find even more sophisticated ways of inflicting pain and suffering on others. Some for the pure thrill of it."

"So that explains why Crown is pushing to have Ray declared a dangerous offender. To keep him off the street as long as we can."

"Yeah, trouble is, that type of sentencing is also generating controversy. Research suggests psychopathic behaviour can be linked to faulty wiring in the brain. That has some people questioning whether psychopaths should be held accountable to the same degree as offenders who don't have these brain abnormalities."

"Jesus, Chris. Owens would have a field day with that twisted logic—capitalizing on the legal loopholes, all the while adding to his list of victims. Yet the longer he's with you guys, the more damage he does with your vulnerable patients like Paul Butler. He's like a fox in a henhouse!"

Chris was tired of talking about Ray Owens and decided to switch to a lighter subject. "That's an east coast accent isn't it, Brandon?"

"Damn straight. Newfoundland, born and bred," he laughed.

"So what brought you out to the other side of the country? Family?"

Brandon went silent. "No, it's just me these days." It was as if a dark memory had started to surface in Brandon's mind, but before Chris could probe further, Brandon quickly changed the subject. "Listen Chris, I was hoping to talk to you about Elizabeth Carrier."

"Have there been any updates on her?"

"No. We issued a statement that tips have been coming in, but no solid leads."

"Ray is connected. He has to be, somehow."

"Yeah, but it's the *how* that we need to prove—with solid evidence. And Chris, I sure could use that cell phone. It might give us the break we've been looking for. Any chance of you going up there with me to locate it?"

"Okay," Chris sighed. "My last visit to Woodland Park didn't go so well. But I'll try again."

The rest of Chris' day was taken up with patient meetings, and he was grateful for the healthy distraction they provided from his dark thoughts of Ray. At five o'clock, as he was getting ready to leave for the day, his phone rang. Call display indicated only that the call originated from the hospital switchboard. He picked up the receiver. "Hey, Ryder. Remember me?"

Chris instantly recognized Ray's voice. "How did you get my number?"

"Give me some credit. How hard do you think it is to get your number, or anyone's number for that matter? Like, let's say, Stephanie Rowe's?"

Chris froze. How did Ray know about Stephanie?

"You still there, Ryder? Or do I have to send a search party out for you?" Ray's laugh was menacing.

"What do you want, Ray?" Chris felt his heart pounding.

"I want a lot of things, Ryder. Starting with my fucking phone."

Chris paused and took a deep breath, not wanting to let on that Ray was getting to him. Then it struck him. Maybe it was time to bait Ray for a change. "Why do you need your phone? It's not like you're going to be needing it anytime soon."

"Don't get smart with me, Ryder. Or maybe my next call will be to your new girlfriend. Goddamn, she's a nice package. Wouldn't that be something if we both fucked her? Then we'd have something else in common." He laughed maniacally.

At the thought of Ray touching Stephanie, Chris panicked. He tried desperately to divert the direction of the conversation. "What makes you think I have the phone?"

"Just how stupid do you think I am, Ryder? I know the cops don't have it 'cause they'd be all over me by now if they did. So that means either you have it or it's still out there on that trail. Either way, you have access to it. So how about we make a deal?"

"What's so important about your phone? Are you afraid

your contacts will incriminate you?"

"Incriminate? Look where the fuck I am. All because of you!"

*Yes!* Chris thought triumphantly. *I'm getting to him. Shot in the dark time.* "Or maybe, Ray, you're afraid your phone will implicate you in Elizabeth Carrier's disappearance?"

"Nice try, Ryder, but I'm not biting. You'll have to solve that one without me. So do we have a deal or what?"

"Why would I want to make a deal with you?"

Ray gave a sinister laugh. "Because I can make your life a living hell, Ryder, that's why. On the other hand, you give me what I want, maybe no one else gets hurt."

"What are you talking about, Ray?" But Chris knew exactly what he was talking about.

"How's your friend Paul? I heard he had an accident."

Chris' face was burning. He wanted to run down to Alpha unit and squeeze the life out of Ray with his own hands.

"Oh, I'm sorry, Ryder. Did I say something to upset you?"

Chris had passed his threshold for restraint and let go with a fury. "I hope—I pray—I get the chance to stand face to face with you again. I'll tear you apart! I swear to God I will!"

Ray responded in a quiet, matter-of-fact tone. "You know, Ryder, when we first met, you looked professional, you spoke professional, and you acted professional. But I knew deep down you weren't that different from me. Listening to you now, I can't tell you how great it makes me feel to hear the changes in you. I—"

"What are you rambling about, Ray?"

"You're changing, Ryder," Ray laughed. "You're becoming more... like me. We'll talk again, real soon. I really feel a connection."

# THIRTY-FIVE

*Friday, February 17, 5:35 p.m.*
As he drove home, Chris was furious with himself for letting Ray get the better of him. He tried to distract himself with pleasant thoughts of this evening's visit with Ann Marie and his date with Stephanie later on. But he couldn't see them in his agitated state. He needed a run before he went anywhere or did anything else.

Running at Woodland Park was not an option. He couldn't even think about that trail without becoming almost paralyzed with anxiety. He'd have to go back there soon to retrieve the cell phone, but it wasn't going to be today. Today's run would stick to the streets of his own neighbourhood.

Chris quickly changed into his running gear, grabbed his iPod, and searched through his playlists until he found the one he was looking for, the one titled "Fuck It All." He pressed play, and the Matthew Good Band began singing about being indestructible. He cranked up the volume and raced out of his building and into the night.

Rain was spitting down and there was a chill in the air, but Chris didn't care. His exhilaration increased with every stride, and he reveled in the sensation of his heart pounding and adrenaline pumping. He felt as if he could run forever. He ran with reckless abandon, dodging cars in busy intersections, oblivious to the frustrated drivers and their honking horns. He worried about nothing and cared about even less. He was invincible!

Nearing his apartment building, Chris felt a magical combination of exhaustion and renewal. This run would rate a strong eight. Now he was ready to take on the world.

Chris put his key in the lock to his apartment entrance only to find that the door was unlocked. He carefully opened it to discover dirty footprints on the hardwood floor. He froze. Someone had been in his apartment. Were they still there? His paralysis broke, and he weighed his options: make a hasty retreat and call 911, or confront the intruder. He chose the latter out of a feeling of personal vulnerability combined with an intense rage that someone had violated his home. And not just anyone. *Ray Owens.* Tiptoeing with his back pressed against the wall, he braced himself for a prowler as he carefully inspected his suite. But he was alone. The contents of his drawers and cupboards were strewn about, but he didn't notice anything missing.

He didn't know how Ray had managed it, but he knew

that somehow the bastard had orchestrated the break-in. Chris knew the wise thing to do would be to report it to the police—Sergeant Ryan came to mind—but he hung up the phone at the last instant. No, this was a personal battle between himself and Ray. Besides, he knew what the intruder was after—the cell phone. He had delayed the inevitable long enough. Chris knew he would have to retrieve the phone.

In his truck on his way to pick up Ann Marie, Chris deliberately shut out the memory of his ransacked apartment and focused his thoughts on his daughter. Friday was not a scheduled day for his visits, so he had been happy when Deanna had extended the offer to him, though he suspected she had plans of her own that evening. Nearing Deanna's house, he noticed an unfamiliar car in the driveway. *Oh my God, he's here.* Memories of the break-in and Ray's threats almost overwhelmed him. But the front door opened, and Ann Marie ran out and down the walkway and jumped into his arms.

Deanna's demeanour was more tentative as she meandered from the living room into the hallway. "Chris... uh, there's somebody I'd like you to meet." Before Chris had a chance to prepare himself, a man he'd never seen before turned the corner and approached him.

"Hi, Chris, I'm Walter." The stranger extended his hand. "Nice to meet you."

"Uh, nice to meet you too." Chris reluctantly shook his hand. He didn't know what else to say. He knew Deanna was dating, but he was uneasy standing inside his former home with the new man of the house greeting him as if *he* were the stranger.

They all stood in awkward silence. Finally Ann Marie brought everyone back to reality. "Daddy, where are we going? Can we go to Wilbur's?"

"Ah, sure, sweetie. Are you ready to go?"

"Mommy, can I go now?"

"Yes, you can." Deanna smiled. "What time will you be back, Chris?"

"I'd say about eight-thirty, Dee. Is that okay?"

"That's fine." Deanna leaned down and kissed her daughter's cheek. "Be a good girl for your father, okay?"

Deanna and Chris locked eyes for an instant, as if both had something they wanted to say but were at a loss for words. Then the moment passed.

"All right, we're out of here. See you later." As Chris closed the door behind him, he wondered whether he should have been more welcoming toward Walter. He paused on the front walkway, contemplating going back to say something friendly to him, before prodding himself onward to his truck. *Forget about it. That was awkward enough.*

At Wilbur's, Ann Marie ordered her standard waffles with strawberries and Chris his scrambled eggs with toast. He listened as Ann Marie talked excitedly about an upcoming birthday party at a Build-A-Bear workshop. Still, he couldn't shake his uneasiness about his experience back at the house. He wondered what Ann Marie thought about Walter and about her mother dating another man. He also wondered how to broach the topic with his young daughter before realizing Deanna had most likely already had that talk with her. In the end, he decided to keep the conversation natural.

"Sweetie, I just want you to know that even though

Mommy and Daddy might become friends with other people, we both still love you very much. You know that, right?"

"I know, Daddy." Unfazed, she corralled the remainder of her syrup. Evidently, this was not as confusing for her as it was for Chris. Still, he thought, it would have been nice if Deanna had let him know in advance that her boyfriend was going to be there. But then again, he reminded himself, he had not yet mentioned Stephanie to Deanna—or to Ann Marie, for that matter. That could wait for another day.

"You know I will always be your daddy, right, Ann?" He realized he was saying this as much for his own benefit as for his daughter's.

"I know. Oh, guess what, Daddy? Mommy said we're going to a movie on Sunday. Walter's coming too. I get to have popcorn and root beer." She squealed with excitement.

"Wow. That's great, sweetie." *Yeah, real great.* His thoughts reverted to his own childhood. His mother had been taken from him when he was a young child, leaving him precious few memories of her. As for his father, his enduring impression was one of emotional distance. Chris had always promised himself that if he ever had children of his own, he would be the best father ever. They would never, *ever* doubt his love for them. Living apart from Ann Marie had never factored into Chris' plan of fatherhood, and the notion that she could have a stepfather was something he hadn't even thought about until tonight. The thought depressed him.

Ann Marie chattered about her friends at school and her favourite television shows. On the ride home, she asked to play her CD and joyfully sang along to "Wheels on the Bus," knowing the lyrics word for word. It struck Chris how quickly his daughter was growing up, which did little to lift his already low mood.

By the time they arrived back "home," Walter had left and Deanna greeted them at the door. Ann Marie filled her mother in on what she had done during her evening, then ran to her room to reacquaint herself with her dolls. Deanna and Chris sat in the kitchen and briefly discussed their daughter's schedule for the week ahead until Chris excused himself and got up to leave.

He had taken two steps out the door when he heard Ann Marie calling for him. He turned around just in time as she ran towards him and threw her arms around him saying, "I love you, Daddy." Four simple words—but they were the most important words in the world to him. Tears streamed from his eyes.

Chris was still flying from Ann Marie's declaration of love as he made his way to Andrea's Café on Seventh Street. Stephanie had suggested meeting at the popular café, and he couldn't help but wonder whether the public setting was a deliberate move on her part in response to their last rendezvous.

No matter, he was looking forward to seeing her wherever she liked and was willing to take things as slowly as required. Entering the buzzing establishment, he spotted Stephanie, her back to him, leaning against the coffee bar. He smiled at the realization that Stephanie stood out effortlessly in any crowd. She wore a black skirt with a slit running up the back, revealing just enough thigh to make Chris ignore every other person in the room. He immediately wished they could go back to her condo and finish what they'd started a few nights

**THE KILLER TRAIL D.B. CAREW**

earlier. Instead, he settled for a gentle hug. "You come here often?" he said with a smile.

Stephanie laughed and gave him a hug in response. "Let's grab a table." She was sipping a latte, and Chris ordered a black coffee. The conversation started out light and friendly. Eventually, he couldn't resist telling Stephanie about the break-in at his apartment, as well as replaying the phone conversation he'd had with Ray Owens.

"He had some nerve, calling me from Alpha unit just to gloat about what he did to Paul." He shook his head in disgust.

"Chris, how about we—"

"And sending someone to trash my place! What a bastard."

"Can we just—"

"I almost wish it *was* Ray and that I caught him in my apartment. I would've loved to smack the smirk off his face. He—"

"Come on, Chris, enough already!" Stephanie slammed her drink down firmly on the table.

Taken by surprise, he replied, "What's wrong?"

"I want to hear about your day, but I really don't want to talk about Ray Owens."

"Sorry. I wasn't thinking. What would you like to talk about?"

"Anything but work, and absolutely *nothing* about Ray. Can we try that?" Chris paused. "You can't, can you?"

"What are you talking about?" he said.

"You're obsessed with Ray Owens. You can't even have a normal conversation without involving him in some way." Stephanie's voice got louder, and her body shook with frustration. "And by the way, I think it's absolutely ridiculous that you didn't call the police about the break-in. That's *their* job, not yours. What's it going to take before you realize you have to let this go, Chris?"

Chris felt his face growing hot. He knew he had to change the topic before the evening deteriorated any further. "Okay. Again, what would you like to talk about?" He attempted a smile that he knew probably looked contrived.

He could tell he'd caught Stephanie off guard, but she quickly regained her composure. "Us."

"Okay, then, let's talk," he said matter-of-factly.

"It's not that simple." Stephanie took a sip of her now-cold latte. "I need to know what you want from this relationship. I need to know where it's headed."

"Jesus, Stephanie, a few days ago you said you wanted to take things slow. And now you want to know where we're headed? That doesn't make sense to me." Stephanie scowled and Chris tried desperately to backtrack. "Uh, what I mean is I... I don't know where this is headed. I'm trying to take it day to day, like you asked. Day to day is fine with me."

Stephanie shook her head in frustration. "That's not what I mean." She paused. "We all have different needs from a relationship. And I think it's only fair to tell you where I'm coming from."

"Okay, I'm listening." *How the hell did we get to this point?*

"I'm not looking for a casual relationship, Chris. I'm turning forty in a few months. I want something with more stability. Something with a future." She paused. "It's funny how we're influenced by our parents. Mine have made no secret of their disappointment that their only child is single and childless. Believe me, they're no role models—they've been separated for years. But it makes me realize I'm reaching a point in my life where I want to settle down." She looked at Chris. "I had hopes that you'd play an important part in my life." She paused, and took a deep breath. "I'm just not sure we're looking for the same thing."

Chris looked at his cup, suddenly wishing it were filled with something stronger than coffee. "I don't know what the future holds, Stephanie. All I know is that I'm incredibly attracted to you and I really enjoy being around you. I always have. Doesn't that count for something?"

"It does. I find you attractive too. I found it very hard the other night to..." Stephanie's cheeks flushed. "But I'm at a point where I have to be selfish about my other needs. I need someone who is focused on me. Not on work, not on somebody else. On me!"

"What are you saying, Stephanie?" But he knew what she was working towards.

"Chris, have you listened to yourself tonight? You're preoccupied with your work, and that's bad enough. Now you're completely obsessed with Ray Owens, and that scares me. It really does. I can't sit idly by and watch you lose yourself in him."

Chris felt his muscles tensing. "That's just not true, Stephanie. I—"

"Please, Chris, let me finish. I can't go on like this. I deserve better." She took a deep breath, then reached out to touch his hand. "I know you don't want to hear this. I know you think I overanalyze everything. Maybe you're right. Maybe it's an occupational hazard for me. But I think you have trouble letting people get close to you out of fear of losing them... like your mother. I feel you're keeping me away."

Chris gave a tired smile. "I knew it would come down to

this. I don't know what else to say because I've been down this road before."

They both looked down at their drinks. The silence was deafening. Chris' heart was pounding. He knew she was right. He could fool a lot of people, but not Stephanie.

Finally, he said in a beaten tone, "So what do you want to do?"

"I really don't know." Stephanie's voice was quavering. She looked to be on the verge of crying. "I don't want to argue like this. Don't you see what's happening to you? You're losing control."

Chris snapped, furious with Stephanie for saying he was losing control— and even more so because he knew she was right. "Fine, you do what you have to do." He pushed away from the table to get up.

"Chris, where are you going?"

"Don't worry about me. I'll survive. Always have— always will." He stood, mumbled a goodbye, and stormed out of the café, wandering aimlessly into the dark night.

Blind to his surroundings, Chris ambled towards his truck, ignoring the rain, ignoring everything but his misery. He didn't see Pierce Hennessy, who'd been watching Chris' every move from the moment he had stepped outside his apartment earlier that day for a run. Nor did Chris detect the man's rapid approach from behind. But he did feel the full impact of the sucker punch that knocked him to the ground. Before he realized what was happening, his assailant leaned down, grabbed him by his hair, and yanked his head off the ground.

The rain smeared the blood gushing from Chris' nose and pooling on his jacket.

His attacker snarled in his ear, "Where's the cell phone?"

Still in shock from the speed of the attack, Chris was confused. "Wha—?"

"The fucking cell phone, asshole. Where is it?"

"I... I don't have it?"

His attacker backhanded him across the face. "Where is it?"

"It's safe." Chris was starting to come out of shock and started thinking about his options. *No matter what else happens, he's not going kill me because he needs me alive to get the phone.*

"Listen very carefully to me." The man prepared to hit Chris again, but was distracted by the sight of a couple heading out of the coffee shop towards them. "You're gonna hear from me again, asshole, and you'd better have that phone. Or I won't be so friendly the next time." To emphasize his point, he left Chris with a parting kick to the stomach before melting back into the night.

The couple approached Chris cautiously. "Hey, man, are you okay? Do you want us to call the cops?"

Chris gingerly rose to his feet. The air had been knocked out of him, and his face hurt. But it was his pride that had borne the brunt of the attack. "I'll survive. Always have—always will."

# THIRTY-SIX

*Saturday, Feb 18, 9:23 a.m.*

Chris woke up with blurry vision and an intense pain radiating from his left cheekbone. A glance in his bathroom mirror confirmed that he looked as bad as he felt, with a nasty-looking black eye and a badly swollen upper lip. On the one hand, he was relieved that it was Saturday and he didn't have to go in to work. On the other hand, the thought of Ray conspiring to have him ambushed infuriated him, and he didn't want to give Ray the impression of having successfully intimidated him. So he popped some extra-strength ibuprofen, grabbed an ice pack to reduce the swelling, and decided to go in to work after all. Besides, he told himself, his irregular work schedule had left him with a number of reports to complete and today would be a quiet day to get them done.

When Chris signed in at the security desk, Horace took one look at him and cringed. "Holy shit. What the hell happened to you?"

Chris thought of using the standard comeback, "You

should see the other guy," until he realized he hadn't even seen much of the other guy, let alone inflicted any damage on him. "I slipped in the shower." He was embarrassed that he'd gotten his ass kicked, something he was pretty sure would never have happened to Horace.

Horace saw that Chris was hurting in more ways than one and decided not to make him feel any worse. "Hey, Chris, I have a feeling the Canucks are going to win tonight. It's only a matter of time before things start going *their* way, you know what I mean? Heck, maybe this is the year they actually take home the Cup."

"Let's hope so. All the same, we could do without another riot if they don't win it all. Talk to you later."

On his desk, Chris found an envelope addressed to him and marked URGENT. *Strange, who would leave an urgent message for me on a Saturday?*

The note read: *Mr. Ryder, you have something that interests me and I have something that will interest you. I suggest we make a deal. Return the cell phone to me and I will return the girl to you. Use the redial function on the phone and await further instructions on how you can be a hero. If you go to the police with this letter, no one will ever see the girl again.*

The envelope had no stamp or return address or any marks that would identify the sender. Chris read the note several more times in an attempt to find some clue that would tell him what he should do next. Again nothing. Chris knew Ray was behind the letter and that he had someone on the outside helping him—someone who had broken into his apartment, someone who had attacked him on the street. *Oh God, someone who might go after Ann Marie or Stephanie!* Chris reread the warning against involving the police. He knew he would be walking into a trap, but he also knew he would never forgive himself if anything happened to Elizabeth Carrier. *Besides, rescuing Elizabeth might be the best way to get rid of the danger to Ann Marie and Stephanie.* The only thing he could do was to return to Woodland Park.

Chris started to leave his office, but at the last minute returned to make a call. Sergeant Ryan answered and Chris opened simply with "Brandon, you've got to trust me on this," and outlined his plan.

Chris drove frantically to Woodland Park. Although he was greatly exceeding the speed limit, it felt like his truck was crawling along the highway. He didn't know what he was going to do once he arrived at the park. He wasn't thinking rationally now. He ignored the voice of reason screaming at him to turn the other way to safety. He was operating purely on instinct. And, not wanting to jeopardize Elizabeth Carrier's safety, he had refused Brandon's recommendation to allow police surveillance in the park, although, in the end, he'd struck a compromise with the sergeant that he would worry about later, assuming he got the chance.

Chris was going to the park completely unarmed and unprepared for what awaited him. He hadn't changed his clothing or picked up supplies, terrified that every second that passed could signal a lost opportunity to save Elizabeth. The only item Chris carried with him was a cell phone charger he'd grabbed from the department's supply cabinet. His mind kept replaying the same mantra: *save Elizabeth Carrier, save*

*Elizabeth Carrier.*

When Chris got out of his Ranger in the Woodland Park parking lot, he was suddenly paralyzed by fear and overwhelmed by a flood of flashbacks. James Carrier's body, its torso partially blown away. The menacing voice at the other end of the cell phone. The iciness of Ray's rifle barrel pressed into his forehead. The crushing feeling of helplessness. Chris felt the familiar pounding in his chest as well as a nauseating anxiety that brought him close to vomiting. Was he walking to his death? *What the hell am I doing here?* Was there still time to turn back and let the police take over? Then he remembered the sorrow he'd felt when he discovered James' body and his sense of duty to prevent another Carrier family member from suffering the same fate.

He took a step forward onto the trail. The cold, grey day threatened snow. His Rockport shoes were no match for the slushy terrain of the park, and within just a few steps, his chinos were splattered with mud.

Although there had been no other cars in the parking lot, he knew somewhere on the trail, a killer lay in wait. And if Elizabeth Carrier was being held anywhere in this park, the most logical place would be the ramshackle cabin where he had sought shelter the evening this whole nightmare started. He saw fresh tire tracks probably made by an ATV headed in the direction of the cabin. He now understood that this was the message behind Ray's taunts about not being out of the woods yet. However, he was the only person aware of the precise location of the cell phone, so he was relatively safe until he had recovered it and contacted his enemy. Then it was anyone's guess if Chris would make it out of the trail alive.

Chris scanned his surroundings as he made his way to the

phone's hiding spot. He was alone on the trail, or at least it felt that way. The crows in the nearby trees were eerily quiet as he passed by but seemed to be watching in anticipation of something. The only sound was the frozen ground crunching under his feet. He was cold and could see his breath in the air, but he knew it was his nerves that accounted the most for his unease as he jumped at the sound of his own footsteps. At last, he reached the location where he had hidden the phone. Taking a cautious look around him, he veered off into the brush to retrieve it.

Using a branch as a makeshift shovel, Chris scratched and scraped at the compacted snow. After several minutes of work, he was rewarded for his efforts. He wiped the snow from the phone's protective case, he marveled at the thought that people were willing to kill over this tiny piece of plastic and electronics. The police wanted the phone as evidence. Ray Owens wanted the phone to keep that evidence secret. And Chris, well, he wanted the phone as a bartering chip to save the life of an innocent person.

Chris' fingers were numb from a combination of cold and anxiety as he hooked the cell phone to the portable charger and pressed the power button. The phone came to life and vibrated in his hand. *Okay. Now what?* He hesitated to press the redial button. *What do I do now?* He was scared. He knew that if he made the wrong move, both he and Elizabeth would be killed. *What's Ray's plan?*

Chris was sure that he'd been ordered to use Ray's phone to make the call because it would confirm that he actually had the phone in his possession. And if Elizabeth Carrier was in fact being held at the cabin, he would be lured there once he made his call. But maybe Elizabeth might be taken to another meeting place in exchange for the phone. In either case, Chris was almost positive that Ray had someone stationed inside the cabin, which meant his greatest chance for success would be to draw Ray's man out into the open.

Chris would use the element of surprise to his advantage. He started running towards the cabin, estimating he would reach his destination in about ten minutes. The cabin finally in sight, Chris chose a hiding spot in the nearby brush. He searched the ground for a makeshift weapon and found a solid branch. *This will do.* He stealthily positioned himself closer to the cabin and noticed the ATV parked in the back. He reached into his jacket for the cell phone and reviewed the phone's outgoing calls. He recognized the one he'd made to Deanna and skipped to the next phone number before hitting the button.

The call was answered on the third ring. "Hello, Mr. Ryder." Chris recognized the voice from his first night on the trail, although he still didn't know the man's identity. His smug voice infuriated Chris.

"I've got the phone. Where is Elizabeth?"

"Where are you, Mr. Ryder?"

"That doesn't matter. Where is Elizabeth?"

"She's safe... for now. That could change if I don't get the phone. *Do you hear me*?" The voice on the other end shouted the last sentence, smugness replaced with impatience.

"I'm still here, aren't I?" Chris took a deep breath to keep his anger in check. He could feel that he, too, was losing control, but didn't want to do anything to jeopardize Elizabeth's safety. "So where do we go from here?"

"I want you to start by answering my question. Where are you?"

"I'm at the entrance to Woodland Park," Chris lied.

"Good. There's an old cabin located within the park. I want you to go—"

"I have no idea what you're talking about. I've never seen any cabin in here, and I sure as hell won't be roaming around looking for it." Relieved that he had guessed correctly where Elizabeth had been hidden, he also knew he was being lured into a trap and he decided to set his own. "I'll meet you in a safe place—right here at the park entrance."

After a brief pause, the voice at the other end responded, "Very well, Mr. Ryder. I'll bring the girl. You bring the phone. Wait there for further instructions from me if you want to see her alive."

From the comfort of his office, C.L. placed a call to Pierce Hennessy, who was stationed in the cabin.

"I've heard from Ryder. He'll be waiting at the park entrance with the cell phone. Bring the girl. But—and I won't repeat this —neither she nor Ryder are to walk away from the park. Is that clear? Good. I'm sending Moyer to help you and your goon with disposal. Call me when it's done."

Hanging up the phone, C.L. breathed a sigh of relief. This mess would finally be cleared up tonight. He'd take care of Ray Owens tomorrow.

Hennessy, too, breathed a sigh of relief as he hung up, happy to finally receive this call from his boss. He'd discovered the cabin while scouring the park for the cell phone and thought it would work nicely as a hideout. But he'd been stuck doing shifts with the Carrier girl for days now and had changed locations a couple times to avoid detection by the cops. He was looking forward to completing the job and collecting his paycheque. He was also still furious that his assault on Ryder the previous night had been interrupted and was looking forward to finishing him off tonight.

Hennessy found the girl enticing in a vulnerable, damsel-in-distress kind of way. He'd tried to have fun with her a few times, and when she had fought off his advances, he'd been tempted to cut her throat. The problem was, he'd been ordered to keep her alive until the job was done. Besides, he figured he'd still have time for fun after finishing off Ryder. In fact, after all the trouble Ryder had caused, killing him would be fun too.

Loading his rifle, he swaggered over to a terrified Elizabeth Carrier. He took the gag from her mouth, removed her blindfold, and untied her from her chair. "Let's go, Princess. Time to roll." He grabbed his duffel bag, opened the door to the cabin and stepped out into the open.

Chris swung the sturdy branch like a baseball bat and connected soundly with a violent thud against Hennessy's head. Caught off guard, the man lost consciousness and collapsed to the ground. Recognizing him from the night before, Chris stood for a moment over his onetime assailant to ensure that he was incapacitated. *Jesus, what have I done?* He'd never carried out such a violent act on another person before, and for an instant, he regretted his action and prayed he hadn't killed the man. The next moment, however, he gave in to the intense pleasure he felt from exacting revenge. "Payback's a bitch, isn't it?" he crowed at his opponent's unmoving body.

He heard weeping from within the cabin. He glanced through the open door at the frightened young woman pressing herself tightly against the wall and realized she had no idea who he was or what was happening. "It's okay, Elizabeth." He battled to catch his breath. "My name's Chris. I'm going to help you get out of here."

Elizabeth appeared to be in a state of shock, her body trembling, the colour drained from her face. Chris was momentarily shaken by her appearance, which was in such stark contrast to the images released to the media from happier times. Gone was the fresh-faced and bright-eyed young woman. Now her clothes were dirty, her hair matted, and her young eyes terrified. Chris feared that her recovery would be long and difficult.

He turned his attention back to Elizabeth's captor lying unconscious at his feet. Entering the shack, he saw a thick rope pooled at the base of a wooden chair that he assumed Elizabeth had been tied to. He pulled the rope outside, tied the downed man's hands behind his back, then dragged him by the shirt into the cabin and tied him to the chair. Finally, he took the rag lying on the floor next to the chair and used it to gag the man.

Chris glanced at Elizabeth who had not moved since his arrival. "It's going to be okay, Elizabeth. We're going home now."

"How... how do you know my name?"

He hesitated, not knowing where to start or precisely

what to say. He elected for the simple truth. "I heard about you in the news."

Tears poured from her eyes. "They killed my father."

Chris resisted the urge to wrap his arms around her to comfort her. After all she'd been through, he wasn't sure how she'd react to being held by a strange man. He struggled to find the right words to say to make it better, but came up empty. Defeated, he softly said, "Are you okay to walk out of here?"

Elizabeth nodded, then suddenly cried out in a panicked voice, "There are other people on the way. I heard him say they'd meet here and then take me to the park entrance."

Chris pulled out the cell phone and called Sergeant Ryan.

"Brandon, I'm at the park and I've got Elizabeth. It looks like Ray's guy is sending reinforcements. I could use some myself right now. We're at the cabin..." He proceeded to bring Brandon up to speed on what had happened, and gave him directions on how to reach the cabin. "We'll hide out in the woods until you get here, okay?"

His call finished, Chris looked around the dim room. Elizabeth's captor had regained consciousness and was glaring at Chris, blood running down his face.

"Remember me?" Chris glared right back at the man. Then he picked up the rifle and gently escorted Elizabeth outside.

After just a few steps, Chris realized that Elizabeth's ordeal had left her in a physically weakened state. Placing his arm around her for support, he knew that their slowed pace meant they would not be able to venture too far from the cabin. He was about to look for a branch to help support Elizabeth's weight, when she cried, "Someone's coming!"

Chris heard movement in the woods and turned his head just in time for a bullet to whiz past him. "What the...?" he shouted and swung around in time to see the shooter reloading his weapon. Grabbing Elizabeth's arm, he dragged her to the front of the cabin, pushed the door open, and shoved her inside, then lunged through the entrance himself as another shot rang out. He fell on top of Elizabeth, but quickly rolled over and used his foot to slam the cabin door closed. They were trapped inside. Chris frantically searched for the rifle that he'd dropped during the chaos and saw it on the floor a few feet away from him. He clutched it and looked at Elizabeth. "Are you okay?"

She nodded, although her quivering body said otherwise.

Chris looked at the cabin's other occupant, who was struggling to free himself from the rope. The man had been waiting all along for his partner to arrive. *What the hell do I do now?* Fragments of plans flashed through his mind. He motioned to Elizabeth. "You keep your eye on this guy," pointing towards her captor.

"His name is Pierce." Elizabeth looked down at him with disdain. "The guy outside is Len."

"Okay. You keep an eye on Pierce. Don't let him get loose. If he moves, hit him with this." He gave her the branch he had used earlier. "I'll handle Len. It's going to be okay," he added.

Chris inspected the rifle. He had never used a gun before so he prayed that just its presence would serve as a deterrent and buy them time. There were no windows in the cabin, and opening the door to search for Len was too risky. He would have to listen for the man's approach and be prepared for the possibility of Len simply charging through the door. He had no sooner finished his thought when a bullet shot through the shack's dilapidated wall.

"Get down, Elizabeth," He shouted as he did the same.

He heard laughter from Len. "Come out, Ryder. Let's play."

"Keep shooting, Len. With any luck, you'll put another bullet in your buddy."

"You're bullshitting me, Ryder," Len shouted. "And what do I care, anyway? It's you I want. You and that cell phone. Where is it?"

"I don't have it. The police do, and they're on their way here now."

"Yeah, I'm sure they are," Len laughed. "Throw it out to me, and maybe we can make a deal."

"I don't think so, *Lenny*."

"You're screwed, Ryder. I can keep you trapped inside there as long as I want."

"So how much is Ray paying you to collect his phone?"

"I don't work for Owens. This goes way higher than that fuckhead."

Chris was confused. "I know you're working with Ray. You're all working together, and you're all going to go down together."

"You got it all backwards, Ryder," Len laughed again. "You don't even know how fucked you are."

Chris frowned. He'd figured all along that Ray was in charge. But if he wasn't, then who was? His thoughts were interrupted by the sound of gunshots echoing in the distance and he guessed they were originating from the park entrance. *Please, God, let it be Brandon and the RCMP.*

"I'm losing my patience here, Ryder. Quit stalling. Throw me the phone and we'll both walk away." Len sounded nervous now.

Fearing Len was planning to barge into the cabin, Chris steadied his rifle and started to shout out to Elizabeth to prepare for his attack but it was too late. Len kicked open the door and shot blindly into the dark interior. For a split second, he stood in the doorway, looking to identify his target in the darkness. It was a split second too long. Chris squeezed the trigger, sending a thunderous blast from the rifle. The impact knocked Len off his feet before dropping him hard on his back.

Chris was in shock. He was sure that Len was dead, when to his relief, Len started writhing in agony, clutching his bloody right shoulder.

"I'm going to fucking kill you!" He clutched his shoulder while feebly reaching for his rifle.

Kicking the rifle away from Len's groping hand, Chris made a threat of his own. "Move another inch and it'll be your last." He needed more rope and found some in Pierce's bag. He wrapped it tightly around Len's body, then dragged Len over to lie next to Pierce.

Chris looked at Elizabeth to make sure she was okay. She was still huddled in the far corner of the cabin, her body trembling in fear. "It's going to be okay now, Elizabeth. Help is on the way." He gave her a supportive smile.

"You're never going to make it out of here alive, Ryder. He'll never let you," Len sneered at Chris.

"Who is this mystery man you keep raving about?" Chris had assumed all along that Ray Owens was the mastermind behind the operation. The thought that Ray was merely a bit player in a larger scheme was unsettling.

"You'll find out soon enough." Len again tried to wriggle free and grimaced in pain with the pressure his efforts placed on his injured shoulder.

"You're right about that one, Len." Chris reached into his pocket, took out the cell phone, and waved it at the bound man. "And *this* will tell me all I need to know about whoever *he* is."

Chris was jolted back to the moment by the sound of a person coming towards the cabin. He reached for the rifle, bracing for another attack. "Who's out there?" he yelled, hoping his angry tone did not betray his fear.

"Is that you, Chris?" Sergeant Ryan called.

"Yes. And Elizabeth Carrier's here with me. And two of Ray's men."

"Is the area secure?"

"Yeah, it's under control." Chris kicked the shattered door off its hinges.

Sergeant Ryan walked into the cabin, assessing the scene before him. He took in Pierce and Len, bloodied and bound, and then Elizabeth, still cowering against the wall, before looking back at Chris, who still held the rifle in his hand.

"I had no choice, Brandon. I had to shoot."

"It looks like you did what you had to do. Good job."

Chris reached into his jacket pocket, retrieved the cell phone, and gave it to Brandon, who stared at it for a moment before commenting, "So this is what all the fuss has been about."

He pulled out his handheld radio and called for an ambulance, giving directions to the cabin. When he was done, he looked at Elizabeth. "It's all over now. You're going to be okay. More police and an ambulance will be here very soon."

Then he took Chris aside. "We picked up another suspect at the entrance to the park. And by the way, you did great work here." He lowered his voice so that he could not be overheard. "But you know we didn't exactly do this by the book. The shit's gonna hit the fan for both of us."

Chris nodded and told Brandon what Len had intimated about Ray having only a minor role in James Carrier's murder and Elizabeth's abduction. "I just don't know who is behind all of this, if it isn't Ray," he said in frustration.

"Yes, but that's where the cell phone comes in. You'd be amazed at how much data we can get from it." Then, walking Chris over to Elizabeth, Brandon took out a notepad and starting asking Elizabeth questions about her abduction.

Within twenty minutes, a horde of police officers and medical personnel on ATVs assembled on the scene. The police cordoned off the area, setting up spotlights around the perimeter of the cabin, which signaled to Chris they would be working well into the night. Pierce Hennessy was handcuffed and taken into custody. Paramedics assessed Elizabeth and Len, then strapped them to modified stretchers attached to separate ATVs that would take them to a waiting ambulance at the park entrance.

At Elizabeth's side, Chris watched the vulnerable young woman. She somehow reminded him of his own daughter, but he quickly pushed away thoughts of Ann Marie being kidnapped. He could only imagine the trauma Elizabeth had been subjected to, and now she would be returning to a world without her father.

As if she had been reading his thoughts, Elizabeth called for Chris to come closer. He leaned down over her stretcher to hear her weak voice. "Thank you." Her eyes were wet, and he could feel his own starting to tear up. He wished there was more he could do or say, but instead simply replied, "I'm so sorry, Elizabeth." She was driven away by the paramedics and a police escort, and he continued to watch in somber silence until she was out of sight.

An RCMP officer approached him. "Mr. Ryder, we'd like you to clear up a few details, including your association with Sergeant Ryan." He proceeded to question Chris, while Brandon stood silently by his side in what Chris welcomed as a sign of solidarity and support.

It was more than a few details, and darkness had fallen before Chris was given the okay to leave Woodland Park. Brandon offered to give him a ride back to the parking lot entrance. Chris shivered, and not just from the cold, as the ATV headlights bobbed up and down, casting ghostly shadows as they reflected off trees and the ground beneath them. Nearing the park entrance, he glanced behind him to take in the park one final time. He had loved these trails. Running them had made him feel alive. But after the death and violence he had been part of over the past few days, he knew he would not be coming back. Still, he felt relief in having conquered his fears and surviving this trail. His thoughts turned to Ray Owens. *I am out of the woods, Ray—you bastard.*

Chris and Brandon reached the Woodland Park entrance, only to find the parking lot transformed into a media carnival.

THE KILLER TRAIL D.B. CAREW

Blinding lights illuminated the entire area, and several media trucks filled the lot and clogged the highway over to the convenience store across the way. Chris was swarmed by a throng of reporters, many of whom he recognized from the local TV stations and the *Sun*. They jostled with each other in a frenetic scrum, while cameras flashed incessantly.

"Is it true you saved Elizabeth Carrier's life? Are these men connected with James Carrier's murder? Did Ray Owens lead you to Elizabeth? Can you comment on..." As microphones jabbed at his face, Chris felt like the main course at a wildlife preserve.

Brandon did his best to shield them both, repeating "No comment" as he elbowed his way, Chris in his wake, through the mob of reporters until they were safely inside his unmarked car. "You're a hero now, Chris. You can expect this kind of reception for the next while."

Chris was speechless, overwhelmed by fatigue and sensory overload. Brandon insisted on driving him home, mumbling appropriately encouraging words in between answering incoming calls on his radio.

When they finally reached his apartment building, Chris thanked Brandon and agreed to talk the following morning. Inside his apartment, he kicked off his shoes, shed his wet and dirty clothes, and collapsed into his bed. Tonight, sleep came quickly.

# THIRTY-SEVEN

*Sunday, February 19, 2:04 a.m.*

Ray awoke with a start from a dream. High in the sky, an eagle was circling, waiting for the perfect moment to attack an unsuspecting and unprotected fawn. Ray knew psychologists would have a field day analyzing his dreams. No doubt they'd say the fawn represented him and somehow they'd try to link the dream to his unresolved feelings of abandonment as a child. He'd heard it all before. He gritted his teeth and scowled. The very thought of people prying into his personal life pissed him off.

His thoughts turned to Chris Ryder. Ray decided to do his own dream analysis, this time featuring himself as the eagle going after his prey. He hoped his elimination of Chris as a threat would finally bring him the peace of mind that had eluded him. *I'm coming for you, Ryder. You're not out of the woods yet.*

## THIRTY-EIGHT

*Sunday, February 19, 10:34 a.m.*

Chris was awakened by sunlight streaming through his blinds. He had slept soundly through the night and well into the morning, oblivious to the fact that his phone had been ringing all morning. A drowsy glance at the alarm clock told him it was past ten-thirty. He scanned his cluttered bedroom but couldn't see the phone. He tottered out of bed in search of it, found it, and saw he had several messages.

He opened his door and picked up the morning's *Sun,* only to stare in amazement at the front-page picture of himself and Sergeant Ryan. The headline read: "Social Worker Saves Elizabeth Carrier*." Jesus, Florence is going to have a fit.* He frantically read the story, which not only identified him by name but also said that he worked at the Institute of Forensic Psychiatry.

The story described the events at Woodland Park that had culminated in the rescue of the young woman confirmed by the RCMP to be Elizabeth Carrier. The article said she had been reported missing several days before, and included a police statement that several persons of interest had been arrested in connection with her disappearance. An RCMP spokesman was quoted as saying that they would not divulge additional information, as the investigation was ongoing. A sidebar discussed the earlier discovery of two bodies at Woodland Park, including that of Elizabeth's father James, and the subsequent arrest of Ray Owens in connection with that investigation. Then came the part of the story that Chris dreaded—the report that Ray Owens had been admitted to the Institute of Forensic Psychiatry, where Chris Ryder was employed. There was no mistaking the *Sun*'s intent of associating Ray Owens with both James Carrier's murder and Elizabeth Carrier's abduction.

Chris stood motionless, staring down at the picture of himself, taken during last night's scrum in the Woodland Park parking lot. He felt sick realizing why he had so many messages waiting for him. He picked up the phone, settled onto the couch, and started playing them.

The first was from a worried-sounding Stephanie, who pleaded with him to return her call ASAP. The next call was from Deanna expressing similar concern. A third message was from a reporter from the CBC asking for an interview. *What the...?* Chris exploded. His telephone and address were unlisted, and he was dismayed—and furious—that he'd been so easy to track down. Not surprisingly, he also had a message from his manager ordering him to call him at home. He was about to contact David when the phone rang again. It was Sergeant Ryan. "Seen the news today? You're a hero."

"Depends on who you talk to, Brandon. My boss doesn't sound too happy."

"No, neither is mine. Unfortunately, that's why I'm calling."

Chris was alarmed. "Do you need me to come down to the station?"

"No, no, nothing like that. At least, I hope it doesn't come to that. I've been in contact with my supervisor. He's pissed that I kept him in the dark about Elizabeth Carrier."

"I'm sorry, Brandon. That's my fault. I'll tell him that."

"No, that's fine. I have no problem taking the heat for that. In fact, in light of some new developments in this case, I think I'll have a solid rationale for my actions. And I have you to thank."

"I don't understand." Chris frowned.

"Our tech guys have been working on the cell phone all morning. Nothing's official yet, but the big news is, we've traced Owens' phone calls. Including the number you called from the park. Ray had him listed as C.L. We're pretty confident we now know who C.L. is."

"Wow, that's great."

"Well, it is and it isn't."

"What do you mean?"

There was a brief pause before Brandon continued. "You have to swear to keep this under wraps, but we think C.L. is Charles Longville, as in the senior aide to the assistant deputy minister with the Ministry of Public Safety and Solicitor General."

It took a moment for the revelation to register in Chris' mind. "How could *he* be connected to Ray Owens? And James Carrier?"

The sergeant sighed. "I know, it's pretty shocking and, believe me, many people are asking the same questions right now. What we know is that James Carrier was researching a story on organized crime for *Maclean's*. It's early stages right now in our investigation, but we believe Carrier uncovered information linking Longville to organized crime. The CFSEU have gone through Carrier's files and are seeking warrants to check out Longville's work and home computers as we speak."

Chris was lost. "Sorry, Brandon, what's the CFS...?"

"CFSEU. The Combined Forces Special Enforcement Unit."

"Never heard of them."

"They're a special task force designed to tackle organized crime. They have staff from the RCMP as well as officers seconded from municipal police forces across the province. They work with other police organizations at the national and international level on organized crime."

"So Longville is suspected of being involved with organized crime? How? I—"

"That's what they're investigating now, but I wouldn't be surprised if it turns out that he's linked to the drug trade. There's a major problem with gangs fighting for control of the drug scene, with cocaine trafficking and marijuana smuggling into and out of Canada and the United States. You've probably been following the drive-by shootings and targeted gang hits in the news over the last several months, yes?"

"Yeah, but to have someone like Longville involved? Wow. That blows my mind."

Brandon didn't respond right away. "Unfortunately, there's more. This has caused huge waves throughout our organization. One of Longville's portfolios includes police services. There's mounting concern that he may have had access to sensitive information from our department. There's even suspicion that someone inside our department has been leaking information to him. That's probably how he found out about James Carrier's story."

Chris felt a sinking feeling in his stomach. He now understood Len's derisive comment about not knowing who he was dealing with. "What a hypocrite! Longville was quick to jump in front of a camera declaring war on organized crime, and all the while he was brokering the deals and lining his pockets."

"Brace yourself. It gets even worse. This has implications for the provincial government. When the media and Opposition get wind of this information, heads will roll. Needless to say, there are a lot of nervous Nellies running around right now, wanting to get to the bottom of this and quickly."

Chris was still puzzled. "But where does Ray fit into all of this?"

"Well, these are early days, and we'll likely know more in the days that follow. But we do know almost for sure that Owens killed James Carrier. Having the call records from his cell phone supports the case that it was a contract hit for Longville."

"Do you think Ray had anything to do with Elizabeth's abduction?"

Brandon paused. "My personal feeling is that he didn't, and we have no evidence to the contrary. I suspect that she was taken on orders from Longville. And the letter you received suggests that she was abducted as a bargaining chip for the cell phone, again on Longville's orders. Of course, proving all of this will take time, but I think the cell phone will go a long way towards achieving this."

Chris felt helpless at the magnitude of the situation.

"What happens next?"

"Well, the department is in panic mode right now, and part of that concerns you."

"Huh? Why me?"

"The top brass from CFSEU, Superintendent Patterson, spoke to my superintendent. Patterson expressed concern that a civilian had no business being involved in a police matter. He alleges you could have endangered Elizabeth's life by not alerting the police at the outset. Of course, by extension that puts me in the hot seat because I didn't share the information you gave me. I met with my boss this morning to try to smooth things over."

Chris was trying to make sense of what he was hearing and the possible consequences for them both. "Am I being charged with anything?"

"Some potential charges have been bandied around. I can't see any weapons charges standing up in court because your use of the rifle can easily be argued as self-defence. They could try to nail you with impeding an investigation, among other things."

Chris felt sick to his stomach. "I guess I'll need a lawyer."

"Let's hope it doesn't come to that, but it's something you might want to look into."

"Brandon, I've really screwed myself, haven't I?"

"I don't know, Chris. I'm sorry to be the messenger, but I thought you'd want to know. Forewarned is forearmed and all that stuff."

"I appreciate it. So what happens with Charles Longville?"

Now it was Brandon who sounded worried. "Remember, you haven't heard anything about this from me, right?"

"No, absolutely. You can trust me."

"I do trust you, that's why I'm telling you. Obviously, our department has to build an airtight case before formally charging Longville. Given the high profile and the evolving nature of the whole Carrier case, I expect Longville to be charged within the next twenty-four to forty-eight hours. I just thought you should know."

"Thanks, Brandon."

"It's not all gloom and doom. Think about the big picture. You saved Elizabeth's life, and you helped solve her father's murder. You're a hero. This other stuff will work itself out."

"I hope so."

Chris returned Deanna and Stephanie's calls. Deanna was out, so he left a brief message saying he would call in the evening to check in and say hello to Ann Marie. Reaching Stephanie's answering machine, he left a message saying he was okay and asking whether she would be available to get together later in the day.

Finally, taking a deep breath, he called his manager. David sounded stressed and demanded they meet in his office the next morning. *I guess I'll find out my fate tomorrow.* He turned on his iPod for a distraction, and R.E.M.'s "Bad Day" started playing. *Tell me about it.*

# THIRTY-NINE

*Sunday, February 19, 2:23 p.m.*

Ray sat in Alpha unit's TV room. He'd claimed the TV remote and was aggressively switching channels, hoping to catch a local newscast to glean additional details about the events at Woodland Park. He'd yelled at two patients when they asked to watch a movie, and they'd wisely picked up on his warning and quickly left the room, leaving him the sole occupant. Still, he was pissed off that he had missed the news hour and the juicy details on how Ryder had managed to avoid being killed on the trail.

Ray was in an all-round foul mood. He knew his time at IFP was coming to an end, and while he would be happy to leave the shithole, he wanted more time to mess with Ryder. He was sure that the police had his cell phone by now and it would be only a matter of time before they made the connection between him and C.L. Not that Ray gave a flying fuck about C.L. or who he was. What he did care about was the prospect of doing more jail time with the evidence the phone would provide. But what infuriated him more than anything else was that Ryder was being portrayed as some kind of hero. *Fucker's stealing the spotlight from me!* He hurled the remote across the room.

*I'll show you, asshole.* The time had come to knock Chris down from his pedestal. Ray was glad he had saved his best shot for last. *This isn't over yet, Ryder!*

# FORTY

*Monday, February 20, 8:15 a.m.*

Chris brewed fresh coffee and ate a couple slices of toast, hoping they would fill the sinkhole in his stomach. He was mentally preparing himself for his meeting with David where he'd have to explain yesterday's actions. The problem was, he wasn't sure he could explain them to himself, let alone his behaviour for the last several days. He suspected that there was nothing he could do or say that would appease David. He'd been ordered in no uncertain terms to stay away from Ray and to keep a low profile. Yet he'd ended up in the middle of a police investigation, with his face plastered on the front page of the newspaper, the rescue as the lead story on every local news channel. Not exactly what he'd planned when he'd set out for a simple run on a trail.

Chris was headed down to his apartment parkade when he remembered he'd left his truck at Woodland Park. Checking the time, he decided to grab a cab to work, which gave him the not-so-welcome opportunity to reflect on the sobering thought that today might be his last at IFP.

The taxi dropped him off in the IFP parking lot. As he walked towards the security desk, his heart sank. Everyone who passed him in the building was staring at him with unbridled curiosity—even Horace, who warmly greeted him with, "Hey, here's the man of the hour."

"Don't know about that." Chris started his dead man's walk to his manager's office. David's door was closed. Chris glanced at his watch and saw that he was on time, so he knocked on the door.

"Come in." The voice from inside the office was not David's. David was not alone; Florence Threader was present too. *Jesus, can things get any worse? Oh well, here comes the special project to Timbuktu.*

Bracing himself to enter battle, Chris saw to his dismay that both Florence and David had copies of the *Sun* strewn across the desk along with a pair of empty coffee cups, suggesting they'd been talking for some time before his arrival.

Florence fired the opening salvo. "Seems you've been a busy boy," she said in a saccharine voice. Her lips quivered with rage. "Did I not make myself perfectly clear that you were to have nothing at all to do with Ray Owens? You do remember that conversation, do you not?"

"Yes. I—"

"Now this morning I hear that, despite my explicit warning, you confronted Owens on a number of occasions. The fact that I am only hearing about this today is profoundly troubling to me—*and* is a matter I have taken up with your manager." She stared intently at an apprehensive David.

"I know. But I can explain."

"I am quite sure you have an explanation for everything. The fact is, however, that from the outset, this was a very sensitive case involving yourself, which is why I ordered you removed. Yet you completely disregarded my authority." She paused to let her words sink in. "You have managed to take an already volatile situation and make it worse. Do you have an explanation for *that*?"

Chris had never seen his director this angry before. He looked at his manager, but David appeared unwilling to make eye contact, as if to say Chris would have to find his own way out of the mess he'd created. He took a deep breath and started to respond, choosing his words carefully.

"I'm sorry, Florence. It's true I had a few run-ins with Ray, but I believe I had no choice. I thought he was behind Elizabeth Carrier's disappearance. He was sending me notes, and I didn't want to turn my back on a chance to help Elizabeth, which—"

"That was an active police investigation. Do you realize I had a call this morning from a Superintendent Patterson asking questions about you? Do you realize you could be charged with a criminal offence?"

Chris swallowed hard. "I think—"

"No, you didn't *think* at all," she snapped. "However, the police can sort out that problem. That's beyond my control. But let me tell you something else that came to my attention from this insightful article in today's paper. I read that your most recent escapade actually started at this worksite, which surprised me, given that you were not scheduled to work on Saturday. I have had security provide me with a printout of your comings and goings at IFP over the last week, and it highlights a number of occasions where you have been here without authorization. As far as I'm concerned, I have grounds for suspending you, although David seems to think you're needed here."

Florence looked at Chris' manager before continuing. "David and I have to discuss this further, and if you incur criminal charges, I won't think twice about terminating your employment. In the meantime, I suggest you keep a very, *very* low profile and do not embarrass this institute any further. Is that clear?"

"It's clear." Chris said in a defeated voice.

David suddenly spoke up to offer support for Chris. "Florence, we'll get this under control. The worst is over now. Mr. Owens will be leaving us, and the press has been portraying Chris in a very favourable light. I'm confident our communications department can put a positive spin on this story."

"We had all better hope so." Florence stood and walked out of the office, leaving Chris and David alone in awkward silence.

Chris took a deep breath and exhaled loudly. His heart rate slowly returned to normal. "Thank you, David. I appreciate what you did. I know you didn't have to, especially after what I've put you through lately."

David took his time to respond. "I know you've been through a lot, and I could tell you were upset with Florence. But you have to realize she's just doing her job." Chris wanted to interrupt him to explain his actions, but decided to hear David out. "In the end, we all report to somebody, and Florence is no exception. The media attention associated with Ray Owens and the Carrier case has placed intense pressure on Florence from the Ministry of Health." He paused for an instant as if pondering the future. "But... well, hopefully this will soon pass."

"I sure hope so." But given what he knew about Charles Longville's association with the "murder at Woodland Park," Chris was not optimistic things would be resolved anytime soon.

Exhausted, Chris left David's office. The thought of being hit with criminal charges *and* terminated employment weighed on his mind. How the hell was he going to be able to concentrate on his work with those twin swords hanging over him? He needed to hear a friendly voice. Stephanie came to mind. He dropped by her office, but she wasn't there, so he decided to try Dr. Stevenson, whom he was glad to find in her office. She was surprised but pleased to see him. "My gosh, you're all over the news. How *are* you?"

"Never better," he said sarcastically. He filled her in on his meeting with Florence. "But other than that, hey, I'm living the dream!" He slumped in frustration. "I don't know what to say. My life sucks right now."

"Sorry to hear that, Chris. The reality is, you saved that girl's life. That's remarkable. You're a hero. Everybody's been talking about you." Chris was about to respond but paused.

Dr. Stevenson picked up on his hesitation. "You want to know about Ray, don't you?"

He smiled. "Was I that obvious?"

"I'm finished the assessment. I've indicated in my report that I have not observed any symptoms of acute mental illness with Ray. I recommend that he be found responsible for his criminal acts."

Chris sighed. "I hear he'll be leaving IFP before his court date."

She nodded. "The sheriffs will be picking him up tomorrow, a week earlier than his court date. Quite frankly, he's too destructive to remain here a minute longer, preying on patients who truly do belong here. He'll wait at the Pre-Trial Correctional Centre. We haven't told him about the early discharge for fear he'll do something dangerous on the unit. That is, something *else* dangerous." Chris silently acknowledged her allusion to Ray's *alleged* assault on Paul Butler. "Our internal review is ongoing, and we haven't had any updates from the police about the assault on Paul."

"The end result is that they'll say the evidence is inconclusive. And Ray will get away with it." He was tired of Ray's games, but he was also running out of the energy he'd need to counter his moves.

"He's a loathsome man. That's the nicest way I can put it, Chris."

He knew if he started to rant about Ray, he'd go on and on, so he decided to divert the conversation. "Any news on Paul Butler's condition?"

Marilyn brightened. "Oh yes. I left a message in your office, but obviously you haven't been back. Paul is doing much better. He was transferred back to us yesterday. He's on Beta unit."

"That's the best news I've heard all morning. I'll drop by to check on him a little later."

"I'm sure he'd like that. I've finished his assessment too. He returns to court next Tuesday. I'm recommending he be considered not criminally responsible on account of a mental disorder. And if the Court agrees and wraps up his case without any undue delays, he could be back with us by the end of next week."

"Good," said Chris, "If that's the case, his mother will likely request a teleconference to go over what happens next with treatment, the Review Board, and so on. I'll check with Paul, and if he's okay with it, I'll call his mother to set up a meeting."

"Sounds good. And Chris, try not to worry about that other stuff. It will work itself out."

"I keep hearing that. I hope so. Thanks."

As he left Dr. Stevenson's office, Chris ran into colleagues who teased him good-naturedly about being a local celebrity. The nurses on Beta unit joshed him about being a hero, and he was starting to become uncomfortable with all the attention. Still, he played along good-naturedly for a few minutes before cutting off their questions and asking if he could see Paul.

Paul was lying on his bed reading a science fiction book. His right eye was still swollen, but he looked better than the last time Chris had seen him. Chris knocked gently on the door frame to announce his arrival. Momentarily startled, Paul broke into a smile when he recognized his visitor. "Hi. Looks like you took a hit in the face too."

Chris smiled back. "Yeah. But your injury was a lot more serious than mine was. How are you doing?"

"I'm all right." There was an awkward pause, then Paul blurted out, "I'm sorry about that whole letter thing. Ray made me swear not to say where it came from. I should have known better."

"That wasn't your fault at all, Paul. I'm sorry about what happened to you. I visited you at the hospital, but you were sleeping."

"Yeah, my mom told me. Thanks."

"Did your mom end up visiting for your birthday?"

"Yes. She went home yesterday. She wanted me to thank you for her, by the way. I think she's planning to call you."

"If it's okay with you, I'll give her a call."

Paul nodded. "Dr. Stevenson says I might be found NCR."

"That's my understanding, too. So if the Court agrees with Dr. Stevenson's recommendation and makes that finding, you'll come back here and we'll help put a plan together for your eventual return home."

"Will you still be my social worker?"

"Yes. Unless you want a different one."

"No, I want you. I can tell you care."

"Thanks, Paul. I'll give your mother a call and set up a time for a family meeting. Sound okay?"

"Yes." As Chris was about to leave, Paul threw in, "I read about you in the paper. You're a hero."

Chris felt his cheeks flush. "It was an... interesting night."

"I'm glad you found that girl."

"Yeah, me too." Chris sensed that there was something else on Paul's mind. "Is everything okay?"

Paul looked anxious and hesitated before responding. "Ray gives this place a bad name. He gives us all a bad name."

Chris was caught off guard by Paul's comment. "What do you mean?"

"I've been reading the paper and the letters to the editor. It's all about Ray Owens and this hospital. People think we're all like him, and they've been saying some pretty crappy stuff about this place." He stopped for a moment, then said in a rush, "The world is hard enough as it is. People look at me differently when I tell them I have schizophrenia. It's hard to get a job, and people won't rent to me. They think I'm going to freak out or something." He took a deep breath. "I didn't know what to expect when I first heard I was coming here. But it's actually a pretty decent place. The staff understands what it means to hear voices, to have a mental illness. And they help. But outside of this place, people think I'm like Ray. And I'm *not*. It just seems so unfair." Paul lowered his head dejectedly.

Chris searched for the right thing to say. He wished he could tell Paul that everything was going to be okay and that the world would understand and accept him for who he was. But he opted for the truth. He placed his hand on Paul's shoulder. "I'm really sorry. You're right. It doesn't seem fair. Hell, it *isn't* fair. I wish I had the answer, but I don't."

Paul looked Chris in the eye. "You don't need to have the answer. We all need to find our own answers. But you helped me by listening and giving me hope. I know I won't be doing it alone." He sighed. "I just wish I'd never heard of Ray Owens."

Chris nodded. "I know what you mean, Paul, I really do." He resisted the urge to continue talking about Ray, deciding instead to discuss things that were within Paul's power. "You're handling things the right way, by focusing on yourself and the things you have control over in your life. That will serve you well. Both here and when you leave here."

"Thanks."

"I'll let you get back to your book. I just wanted to come by to say hi. I'll see you tomorrow."

Chris headed to his office. Over the past few days, he'd spent very little time at his desk, and knew his colleagues in the social work department had been picking up the slack—taking on new patients admitted for court-ordered assessments normally assigned to Chris, as well as dealing with his current patient caseload.

He'd owe the team big time when things settled down. Of course, his days at IFP might be numbered. He would miss his colleagues, both within the department as well as throughout the hospital. He'd had many ups and downs over his years at IFP, but this was the best place he'd ever worked, and he considered many of his co-workers the closest thing to family he'd ever known.

He tried to shake the depressing thought from his mind and focus on something constructive. Glancing at his watch, he saw that he was late for the social work department's weekly staff meeting, debated whether he should attempt to catch the last ten minutes, unsure how his colleagues would receive him after his behaviour of the past few days. But he decided it was important to offer his apologies and extend his thanks to the rest of the department, particularly if this was in fact his last working day.

Four of Chris' colleagues were sitting inside the room, with no sign of his manager. He walked in and sat down. "Hi guys, sorry I'm late." Whatever topic had been on the table before his arrival was abruptly dropped, and all eyes turned to him.

*I guess the floor's mine. Where to start?* He thought for a moment, then decided to keep it simple and start with the truth. "I... I came here to say I'm sorry. Feels like I've been saying 'I'm sorry' a lot lately. The last week or so has been like a roller coaster for me. Anyone who knows me knows I don't do well on roller coasters."

Allison smiled. Heartened, he continued. "Believe me, I would never have chosen to be in this situation. I feel like I got dropped in the middle of it. I've been trying my best to fight my way out ever since." He could feel by the lump in his throat that he was on the verge of losing control. "I know I've made mistakes, and I know I've left you in the lurch and stuck picking up after me. So again, I'm sorry." He wasn't sure what else to say, so he stopped.

"You don't have to apologize," Katherine said softly. "We know you've been going through hell. We've all been really worried about you."

Sarah joined in. "If anyone should be apologizing, it's us. We've felt bad because we've wanted to do something to help but we didn't know what to do."

"Yeah, don't worry about us," Gerald piped up. "We know you've been kinda busy lately. Saving lives and gracing the front page of the *Sun.*" Gerald's comment elicited real laughter from the group, dispelling any lingering tension.

Chris took a deep breath. "Yeah, well, about that. This hasn't gone over well with David. And Florence is really pissed at me right now. I'm not sure how it's going to end— whether I get suspended or fired. I wanted to tell you that I really appreciate you guys."

"They can't do that, they're full of shit!" Gerald protested. His colleagues reacted with similar dismay and Chris assured them he'd keep everyone updated on his status. He stood up to leave, and Allison walked over and gave him a hug.

"They'll come to their senses, Chris, realize you're too good to let go," Sarah offered.

Then Gerald told him to sit down again and demanded the juicy details about the rescue at Woodland Park. Chris could tell that the rest of the team was also interested. "I'm sorry, but much as I'd like to tell you my story, it'll have to wait for another time. You know it's still part of an active police investigation." *Who am I fooling?* The fact of the matter was that he was too physically and emotionally drained to revisit his misadventures at the park. But he took comfort from the fact that he was leaving on good terms with his colleagues as he headed back to his office.

Chris found a temporary respite from his problems by focusing on his work, mostly interviews with patients and returning phone calls to their family members. He was about to take a break when he received a call from Sergeant Ryan.

"I wanted to let you know that we're closing in on collecting enough evidence to arrest Charles Longville for his part in the murders at Woodland Park."

Again Chris flashed back to James Carrier's gruesome murder, and the possibility of criminal charges being laid against him amplified his feeling of despair. But he realized he was not alone, that he and Brandon were in this situation together. Brandon was surely catching as much hell from his superiors as Chris was for holding out on the investigation. "How are you doing, Brandon?"

The sergeant said, "Well, our department has become a circus, and it's going to get even crazier when the media get wind of Longville's connection. But I'm hanging in there."

"So the cell phone helped, did it?"

Brandon laughed heartily. "That phone blew this case wide open. It's no wonder people were willing to kill for it. Our IM/IT guys have been having a field day with it." He proceeded to fill Chris in on what the RCMP had extracted from the phone in terms of telephone numbers and contacts. "So that's my story. Now, how are things at your end?"

"Not so good." Chris filled Brandon in on his meeting with his director and her threat to fire him.

"Nah, I can't see them following through on that. C'mon, the way the media's singing your praises about the Carrier case—that's got to be great PR for IFP. By the way, I followed up with Elizabeth today. She seems to be doing okay, all things considered. She asked me to say hello to you."

"That's a bit of good news for a change."

"It *is* good, which is my point. Your role in saving Elizabeth has been the one feel-good part about this whole tragedy. That's why the media have run with it. If your top brass have any brains at all, they'll see that it would be stupid to let you go at a time when people are celebrating you."

"God, I hope so. Guess I'll have to wait and see."

The sergeant's voice became serious. "Apart from that, I've got good news and bad news. Which do you want first?"

Chris' thoughts jumped immediately to the possible criminal charges hanging over his head and his heart started pounding. He found himself unable to respond. Brandon picked up on his silence. "Okay, I'll start with the good news. I don't think anyone within our department or the CFSEU is going to pursue charges against you. There's nothing that would stick and there's too much of a risk that it would bring unwanted attention to the bigger story—the Longville connection and the possibility that we had someone inside leaking information to him. So I suspect they'll blow some hot air at you, but nothing more."

Chris sighed with relief. "I hope so. I just want to put this whole thing behind me—Ray Owens, Charles Longville, everything. And get on with my life."

"Yeah, the spotlight is certainly shining on you right now. But the next big story is always around the corner. Then they'll forget all about you and move on to someone else. I would say Longville may be that person. Anyway, I just thought I'd give you a heads-up."

"Thanks." Chris braced himself. "What's the bad news?"

"From what we're learning about Longville's involvement with organized crime, the sooner we have him in custody the better, because he's extremely dangerous. Especially when he realizes that we have the phone. He'll know you're a witness, so there's a good chance he may go after you."

"Jesus! What about my family?"

"Hold on, I was getting to that. Ironically, you can probably expect a call from CFSEU. They'll likely offer you police protection, and if they don't, we will."

"Great. And I thought I only had Ray to worry about."

"You raise an interesting point, actually. Longville hired Owens. If Owens talks, that makes him a threat to Longville. I wouldn't be surprised if Longville goes after him too. Hopefully we'll have enough evidence to charge Longville soon. In the meantime, be careful."

"I will, and thanks. And by the way, when all of this is over, I'll buy you a beer."

Brandon laughed. "I'll hold you to it, buddy."

At five o'clock, Chris was getting ready to leave work when his manager appeared at his door. "I'm glad I caught you."

"You wanted to talk with me?"

"I wanted to check in and see how you are doing. That wasn't a pleasant meeting this morning."

"I've had better." *So what's the verdict? Will I have a job tomorrow?*

"I've been talking with Florence. We've been preparing briefing notes for our communications department. They'll be releasing a statement to the media concerning this whole mess with Ray Owens, including your involvement with Elizabeth Carrier and, by extension, the involvement of IFP."

He paused, appearing to deliberate on the best way to continue. "Florence wanted you fired, or at the very least, suspended indefinitely."

"I know." *Here it comes.*

"I told her I wouldn't support your dismissal."

"You did *what?*" Chris couldn't believe what he was hearing. No one second-guessed Florence, and he never would have expected David to put his own neck on the chopping block after what Chris put him through. "I don't understand. Why?"

"It comes down to what I see as the best interests of our department. I told Florence that you are too valuable an asset to this department and your departure would be a significant loss."

"And she agreed with you?"

"She wasn't happy, but she's a smart woman. She knows the union would strongly back you up, and the optics of a dismissal right now would look bad if the media caught wind of it."

"I don't know what to say. Except thank you."

David gave him a stern look. "Don't confuse this with me condoning your actions. You landed us both in serious trouble. Quite frankly, I don't know that I'd be as able to help you in the future. So please, for Christ's sake, don't put me in a position where I have to. And please, for crying out loud, stay the hell away from Ray Owens."

Chris nodded. "I'll do my best. I really will."

"Good. Well, that's all I came to say." He took in Chris' haggard appearance. "No offence, but you look terrible. Go home. Do yourself a favour and take tomorrow as a sick day and get some rest. Okay?"

"Okay. Thanks again, David. I mean it."

# FORTY-ONE

*Monday, February 20, 5:25 p.m.*

Chris called a taxi to take him to Woodland Park to collect his truck. A pleasant exhaustion overtook him as he sat back and enjoyed the ride. Aside from annoying questions from the driver, who recognized him from the news and couldn't resist asking about the case, Chris was free to take in the sights around him. The sun was setting on a splendid day, turning the sky a stunning shade of orange. For the first time since he'd encountered Ray Owens, his heart did not race in terror as he entered the park. Still, he was happy to retrieve his truck and put the trails behind him.

He drove back leisurely to his apartment with a feeling of contentment. He wasn't sure how he was going to spend his evening. He hadn't heard back from Stephanie. Still, he was happy enough to stay in and while away the hours listening to music.

The phone rang, interrupting his musical interlude, and Chris briefly considered ignoring it and the outside world for the night. But, hoping it might be Stephanie, he picked up.

"Hey, Ryder, sounds like you're partying and didn't invite me. What gives?"

At first, Chris was confused. *This can't be Ray. He doesn't have my number.* Then he remembered Ray would have discovered his address when he'd first rifled through his truck. Chris clenched his fist in an effort to suppress his rage.

"What's the matter, Ryder? Cat got your tongue? Or is the big shot Ryder too good to take my calls?"

"What do you want, Ray?" he said through gritted teeth as he got up to check to make sure the door was locked.

"I saw you on the news, Ryder. They're calling you a hero. What a joke. I just about shit myself when I heard that."

"What do you want? Answer me, or I'm hanging up."

"I bet you think you won," Ray sneered.

"What are you talking about?"

"Me!" Ray shouted. "You! I bet you think you beat me."

"Listen carefully, Ray. I wasn't thinking about you at all. And after I hang up, I won't be thinking about you. You'll be gone. In the past."

Ray snickered. "That's what I'm calling about, Ryder, the past. You tried digging into my past when I was at your shithole hospital the first time. But you didn't get very far, did you?"

"I don't know what you're rambling on about. What's your point?"

"The *point* is, I had this nosy probation officer about six months ago doing the same fucking thing—digging into my past. Turns out she had dug up a report on me from Social Services from years ago, but the bitch wouldn't share it with me. So I paid a visit to her office one night and took the liberty of making my own copy. It was... how should I say? Enlightening." He laughed.

"Why are you telling me this? Are you lonely or something? Got no one else to talk to in your pathetic little world?"

Ray ignored Chris' jibes. "Most of the report was boring as shit. Didn't tell me anything I didn't already know. Anti-social this and anti-social that. But there was one detail that caught my eye—my old man's name."

"So what? Are you telling me this because you want me to understand you? Is that your point?" *Is he suicidal?* Chris almost laughed at the thought. *I should be so lucky. But there has to be some motive. What is it?*

"Turns out my old man liked to drink, gamble, and fuck—a lot." Ray laughed. "Just like me. I never met my mother—probably some skank the old man fucked out of boredom. No one could track her down after I was born, and the old man couldn't care less. So they put me in foster care. But listen to this, Ryder, cause this is where it gets real interesting. The report said he fucked this other bitch—Fiona something or other—and got *her* pregnant, too. Had a son."

Chris felt his face burning, his heart pounding. He couldn't breathe, and ringing in his ears almost drowned out Ray's next taunt.

"Take a guess at the name of my father, Ryder."

*No! Please, God, no! This can't be happening!* Chris was gripped by panic.

"Maurice Fucking Ryder."

*No! It can't be!* Chris tried to run through alternate explanations to counter what Ray was saying. *Please, God, don't let this be true!*

Ray's voice intruded. "It's like we were meant to find each other, Ryder. What do they call that? Fate?" He cackled. "I call it a fucking gift, and I'm gonna have fun with it. We'll talk soon. We have unfinished business... *brother.*"

The line went dead.

In shock, Chris remained standing in the middle of his living room. *It can't be true. Ray could easily have uncovered information about my father.* But he knew there was only one person who could set the story straight—his father Maurice. He'd have to see him. Tomorrow, he decided with trepidation. *I will survive this.*

# FORTY-TWO

*Tuesday, February 21, 8:58 a.m.*

Even after a few drinks, Chris slept fitfully through the night. His mind kept replaying the conversation with Ray, always returning to his pending visit with his father. Several times during the night, he considered aborting his plan to visit Maurice, but he knew deep down that he couldn't, that he had to know the truth about Ray.

Night gave way to a beautiful sunny morning and Chris woke to the joyful sound of birds chirping outside his apartment building. He lumbered out of bed and prepared for the drive ahead of him. His stomach still in knots, he skipped breakfast, figuring he'd grab a coffee once he hit the road.

The bright point of Chris' day would be visiting his Aunt Mary, whom he'd called the night before. She had heard about him in the news and was relieved to talk with him and know first-hand that he was okay. It had been several months since he'd spoken with her, and he felt guilty that he did so little to maintain contact. Mary confirmed to the best of her knowledge that Chris' father was still living in the same dilapidated house. She made Chris promise that he would drop in to see her before he went to visit Maurice.

Mary had become Chris' surrogate mother after her sister Fiona's death. She had always wanted children of her own, but life hadn't been kind to her in that regard. Never one to feel sorry for herself or to turn her back on someone in need, she moved to be near Chris after his mother's murder. She knew enough about Maurice's drinking to realize that she couldn't leave her nephew in his hands, so she raised Chris in her own home. She did everything within her power to nurture a bond between father and son. She invited Maurice to special occasions including birthdays and Christmas, and she sent regular updates on his progress in school. Her efforts were in vain; Maurice remained apathetic towards his son's existence and indifferent to the assistance Mary provided.

When she felt he was old enough, Mary told Chris about his mother—what a wonderful human being she had been and how she had lived her life helping other people. Mary had tried to spare him the details of the tragic way his mother had died at the hands of a cold-blooded killer, but the boy became obsessed with reading newspaper clippings about the hostage incident at the hospital where Fiona had worked, which had ended in her death.

Mary never talked disparagingly about Maurice, despite having ample opportunity to do so. As he grew into his teens, Chris tried to connect with his father, yearning for a bond. But his efforts, too, were in vain.

As an adult, Chris' only family connection was his aunt. He felt a combination of nostalgia and sadness as he pulled up to her street and into her driveway.

Mary greeted Chris with a big hug, then grabbed his hand and pulled him into her living room. He'd always considered her to be a strong woman in body and mind and was relieved to see that while her body looked fragile now, her fiery spirit remained intact.

As soon as they were seated, she began to cry. "Oh, Chris, it's so good to see you in one piece. I was so worried when I read about you."

"It's good to see you too, Auntie. You're looking as young as ever."

She laughed and wiped her eyes. "Silly boy, I don't feel young these days." Then she smiled. "And look at you. You're no longer a boy. But enough about our age, let me get you something to eat."

"No, no, Auntie, I'm fine." But even as he spoke, his aunt was up and walking towards the kitchen. She returned with a plate of homemade cookies and pastries.

"These look great," he mumbled. "Just like the old days. Thank you, Auntie."

"I baked the brownies this morning. I remember they were your favourite." Aunt Mary had always taken pride in her role as hostess. Chris wondered how many visitors she entertained these days. Probably not many—which left him feeling sad for her and angry with himself.

"Auntie, I'm sorry it's taken me this long to see you. I know Ann Marie would love to see you too."

"Well, you're here now, and that means the world to me. Of course, that lovely daughter of yours is always welcome here."

"I know, and I promise we'll both be in to visit you soon." He took a bite of a brownie. "Wow. They taste just the way I remember. Maybe even better. Can I take a few for the road?"

"Of course you can, dear boy." But her cheery mood turned somber as she remembered the reason for her nephew's visit. "So you're here to see *him?*" It was obviously a rhetorical question, but Chris nodded anyway. "Just don't expect much from that man. He'll only disappoint."

"It's okay. I'm not expecting much. I just have a few questions to ask him and then I'm on my way." He smiled. "You, Auntie, are the social part of my visit."

His aunt frowned. "What kind of questions would make you drive all the way out here to see a man who's never had the time for you?"

He didn't want to burden her with what Ray had said, but he also knew he couldn't lie to her. He sighed deeply. "I need to know whether I have any brothers or sisters."

He watched her face turn pale. "You're the only child your mother had."

"I know, Auntie." He paused for an instant. "But I need to know whether my father had any other children... with... well, with anyone else."

Mary sat back in her chair. Chris wasn't sure if she was confused or upset, but either way he felt bad for putting her in this position. Finally, she said, in a voice so soft that he had to lean forward to hear her, "That man has a history that you are far better off not knowing. Do you hear me?"

"It's okay. I'm not looking to know every little thing about him—just one detail."

"Why do you need to know?"

"It'll help me with something I'm working on. It's not

dangerous or anything like that." He mentally crossed his fingers at his lie. Anything related to Ray was inherently dangerous.

Mary took a long, hard look at him as if trying to read his mind. A tear ran down her cheek, followed by another. "Your mother would have been so proud of you." She wiped her face. "She only wanted the best for you, Chris, and I made a promise that I would do everything I could to help when she was... when she was taken from us." She paused and took a deep breath. "If you ever want to talk about your mother, Chris, I'm here for you."

For years, Chris had taken pains to block out memories of his mother. Yet he knew he would have to revisit that part of his life to prepare himself for battle against Ray.

"Auntie, you're responsible for any good that's in me, and I appreciate all the support you've given." He took a breath and looked away from his aunt to keep from breaking down.

She smiled faintly at the compliment even as tears continued to stream down her face. "There were times when it was touch and go, when I thought I was going to lose you. You suffered such terrible nightmares. You wouldn't talk about them. All you'd say was that it was about the bogeyman."

Chris didn't have the heart to tell her that the bogeyman did in fact exist.

"You'd retreat to some dark place in your mind. I couldn't follow you there. I'm so sorry, Chris, so sorry. I could feel you were troubled, but I couldn't do anything. You wouldn't talk to the child therapist." Wiping her tears away, she paused for a moment. Finally, she said somberly, "Please, Chris, I beg you, stay away from those places. You have to fight the darkness."

As he left his aunt's house, Chris braced himself for his visit with his father. As far as Mary knew, Maurice still lived alone. Chris hadn't seen him in nearly two years, and the last visit hadn't gone well: it had finally forced him to realize that his father had never cared for him and, despite Chris' efforts, never would. But now Chris was no longer reaching out to his father. He needed information from him, plain and simple, and once he had it, he'd eliminate the man from his life once and for all.

He was driving to his father's house when his cell phone buzzed. Stephanie. He desperately wanted—*needed*—to hear her voice, but he didn't want to burden her with his problems. He also knew she would try to talk sense into him to turn away from this newest confrontation. He ignored the call.

Chris knocked tentatively on his father's door, then more forcefully, then repeatedly. No response. The house was even more run-down than the last time. He suspected he could barge through the rotting doorframe with little effort and was contemplating whether this would be necessary when the door creaked open and Maurice stood before him.

The passing of time had not been kind to Maurice. His face was gaunt and covered with several days' worth of scraggly stubble. His sparse grey hair hung in lank, greasy strands. Disheveled, dirty clothes drooped loosely on his scrawny frame, and he reeked of alcohol.

He gave Chris a tired look. "Well, if it ain't the hero.

You've come a long way here, boy, when a call could have done the same."

*Nice to see you too.* Chris contemplated how he was going to broach the subject of Ray. "Would you have answered the phone?"

His father gave a sly smile, exposing dirty yellow teeth. "Probably not."

"Can I come in?"

"Suit yourself." Maurice turned and shambled back into the living room. Chris followed. The interior of the house was much the same as he remembered from two years before. The living room stank of body odour and stale smoke. Papers and empty bottles littered a threadbare carpet of indeterminate colour. A small television showing the movie *Die Hard* blared in the centre of the room. Maurice retreated to his tattered recliner and, ignoring Chris, stared at the screen. *Yeah, just like old times.*

Chris looked around the dim room for a chair that wasn't covered in debris and didn't appear too rickety. Finally finding one that he figured might hold his weight, he moved it next to his father. "You're right, I could have called. I did call Aunt Mary to make sure you were still here."

"Mary, huh. So the cow's still kicking around." He turned to look to Chris. "What're you doing here, anyway?"

"Yeah, I guess I'll get right to it." Chris hesitated. He wasn't sure he'd like the answer to the question. But he needed to know. "Is the name Ray Owens familiar to you?"

He watched for a reaction, some recognition of the name. Nothing. His father simply shrugged. "No. Should it be?"

Chris wished desperately that this meant that Ray had lied, that there was no blood connection between the two of them, but he knew he had to dig deeper.

"The last name 'Owens' is an adopted name. But he was named Ray or Raymond when he was born."

"What does this have to do with me?" Maurice said with annoyance..

"He says you're his father."

"Well then, he must be right. There, mystery solved."

Chris could feel himself losing patience. "It's a simple question, Maurice." He couldn't bear to call this excuse for a man "father," not to his face. "Is Ray Owens your son?"

Maurice paused for a minute, and Chris saw what looked to be a small flicker of recognition in his face. "Yeah, I guess he could be."

"Look Maurice, I'm not trying to put words in your mouth. I just want to know whether he's your son or not."

Maurice scowled. "What's it to you, anyway?"

"I'm trying to see if someone is messing with me or telling the truth."

"Oh, I get it. This is connected to your little adventure in that park, isn't it?"

Chris clenched his hand into a fist. "So you're not really sure whether you had another child, other than me?"

"I didn't say that." Maurice took out a pack of cigarettes, lit one, and took a drag. "Yeah. I had a boy before you. A little runt, as I recall. They named him Ray. I sure as hell didn't name him that. His mother disappeared, and I wasn't prepared to take him, so Social Services took him. That's all I know."

*It's true. Ray is my half-brother.* Chris felt as though he'd been punched in the stomach. He struggled to breathe. Oblivious to Chris' discomfort, Maurice placed his cigarette on a makeshift ashtray overflowing with butts, reached down the side of his chair, and pulled up a bottle of Captain Morgan. He poured a generous amount into a glass sitting on the table next to him. He reached for his no-name cola and, seeing that the bottle was empty, looked to Chris.

"Do me a favour, will you? Grab some pop for me. There should be one in the kitchen."

*Some things never change.* Chris picked his way through the mess to the kitchen. Food-encrusted dishes littered one counter, while several grocery bags were strewn along another. He searched through the bags before finding a bottle of cola. He made his way back to the living room and slammed the bottle down on the table next to his father. Maurice splashed some cola into his glass of rum.

"Are you working these days?" Chris asked, sure he already knew the answer. Maurice had always had a spotty work history with only brief stints at the local sawmill.

"What? No, no. I'm on disability for my back. It needs rehab." Maurice turned back toward the television.

*Liquid therapy, most likely.* "Well, I'll be on my way." It was obvious his father wasn't interested in talking any further, and neither was he.

"Suit yourself." Maurice took a swig from his glass, indifferent to Chris' presence. *The story of my life.*

"I'll let myself out. Don't worry about me." He was almost through the front door when he felt a massive rage building in him. He couldn't leave yet. Storming back into the house, he planted himself in front of the television set, ensuring he had Maurice's attention. "You don't give a damn about anything, do you?" Chris could feel his anger rising, but he knew he was desperately close to breaking the one cardinal rule his father had instilled in him as a child—never cry in front of another person. He fought to hold back the tears, but it was a losing battle. And now he was furious with himself too, for exposing his vulnerability in front of his father.

Maurice sat silent and motionless.

"Goddamn you, Maurice, you're the reason I feel ashamed to cry, the reason I'm emotionally fucked up. You told me I was weak to cry. That's the one thing from you that's lasted with me all my *fucking* life."

Maurice listened impassively to his son's tirade. Chris took a deep breath and said in a calmer voice, "You really don't feel anything do you? You're a ghost. That's all you've ever been to me." Angrily wiping away his tears, he looked his father in the eye and said with disgust, "You don't have anything at all to say, do you?"

Maurice took a long drag on his cigarette and, without looking at Chris, said, "Cry me a river."

Chris clenched his fists, wanting to pound the shit out of his father. He stopped himself at the last instant. Instead, he cleared his throat and said, "The next time I see you will be at your funeral. And I promise you, I won't shed a tear. You'd be proud." He slammed the door behind him.

Not looking forward to the monotonous drive home, Chris thought about booking a room at a local motel, but decided against it. He had an even greater desire to get as far away as possible from Maurice. The filthy state of his father's house had repulsed him, but he was more sickened at the sight of his father's baneful existence. For too many years, he had turned a blind eye to who and what his father was. He'd always given

Maurice the benefit of the doubt and had even made excuses for him. Today, however, he saw the man for who he really was. And it disgusted him.

What he found even more profoundly disturbing was sharing DNA with Maurice. And Ray. Two men he despised. This sickening revelation changed the way Chris even looked at himself. His biggest fear had always been that he was not that different from his father. *I even drink the same brand of rum. But I'll never, ever treat Ann Marie the way he treated me.*

Chris' thoughts turned to Ray, his half-brother. *The same blood runs in me.* He shuddered. He wondered if the rage he felt inside him might make him capable of the same horrific acts as Ray.

*I am not my past.* But the doubts lingered. *Am I really that different from Maurice? From Ray?*

# FORTY-THREE

*Wednesday, February 22, 3:54 p.m.*

Ray sat in his cell, fully alert. It had only been a few hours since he'd been discharged from IFP and admitted to the Pre-Trial Correctional Centre to await his court date, but his instincts told him that something big was about to go down. He saw it in the way the other inmates looked at him and went out of their way to keep a safe distance. He'd seen this reaction when he'd been incarcerated before. It signaled that someone was about to be shanked. And he sensed that someone was him.

He was not being targeted because of the crimes he'd committed; guys in this shithole were charged with way more heinous crimes. Nor was he marked because his case had been in the media. He recognized an inmate he'd read about just recently—a gangbanger who'd killed a six-year-old girl during a botched drive-by shooting. No, Ray figured there was a price on his head for an altogether different reason. He was certain C.L. was behind it.

Ray didn't know who C.L. was, and he'd never given a

second thought as to why his marks needed to be killed. Now that he was almost certainly on the receiving end of a hit, he had to admit he'd underestimated C.L. He would definitely make a point of researching his bosses in the future. Right now, however, he had to deal with the present danger.

He didn't know when the attack would occur, but he planned to be ready for it. He casually walked over to the toilet in his cell, dropped his pants and sat down as if to take a shit. He was careful, though, as this "shit" involved extracting a foreign object from his rectum. When he was through, he was the proud owner of a sharpened half-toothbrush he had secretly removed from IFP. It would serve nicely as a makeshift weapon. Sitting back down on his bed, he smiled broadly, trying to anticipate his unknown opponent's next move. He liked this game.

The attack went down as the inmates were gathering for supper. Ray didn't recognize his attacker—just the telltale parting of the crowd making way for a lone assailant who rushed him with something concealed in his left hand. Ray deftly shifted his position, averting a stab wound, and as the two men clashed, Ray thrust his weapon deep into his foe's neck, snarling, "Better luck next time, asshole." He had wanted to target the eyes but would settle for a neck wound any day. His would-be attacker writhed in pain on the cold prison floor, helplessly clutching at his neck as blood pooled on the floor. Alarms sounded, additional guards rushed in, and the cellblock was locked down. Ray was thrown into segregation, but he didn't care. C.L. had tried to send him a message, and Ray had sent a message of his own. *Nobody fucks with me.*

**THE KILLER TRAIL D.B. CAREW**

# FORTY-FOUR

*Wednesday, February 22, 3:54 p.m.*

Driving back home, Chris mulled over what he'd discovered about Maurice and Ray. Ray had gleaned *his* information about their family history from the Social Services records collected by his probation officer. Now he too needed to see those records to learn as much as he could about his connection to Ray. Getting access to the files, however, would not be easy. Not only would Chris be breaching ethical and professional standards, but there could also be legal consequences if he was caught. Nevertheless, he felt he had no choice in the matter. Every fibre of his being told him that Ray was determined to go after not only him but also those close to him. Chris was equally determined to prevent that from happening.

He thought briefly of asking Gerald to request Ray's records, but no, he didn't want to involve his friend in his clandestine ploy. Next he considered his contacts at the Ministry of Child and Family Development and at the Adult Community Corrections Branch. Yes. It would probably be easier to get the files from a probation officer at the corrections office.

Pulling over to the side of the road, he dialed a familiar number. Mason Jean, a probation officer who had worked with Chris on many cases over the years, answered the call. "Hey, Chris, I keep reading about you in the *Sun*. Talk about work hitting close to home. How the hell are you?"

"Oh, I'm fine. Never a dull moment around me, you know."

"So what can I do for you?"

"Well, you probably know that Ray Owens has been at IFP for assessment, right?"

"He's been hard to miss. It's like the two of you are competing for airtime."

Chris ignored the wisecrack. "I understand he's had some past involvement with your office. It would be great if you could send me what you've got—pre-sentence reports, probation orders, even records from MCFD that you have on file. That would help us out a lot."

There was a moment of silence as Mason checked his computer to locate Ray in his system before responding. "Sorry, man, his file is closed with us right now. It looks like Mildred worked with Owens last. I can let her know you called and have her get back to you."

"Actually, Mason, I was hoping you could help me. If I talk with Mildred, she'll ask me for a signed consent from Owens, and we both know he'll never give us that. We're seriously under the gun to finish our assessment in time for his court date. Are you sure you couldn't help me out?"

"Gosh, Chris, you're putting me in a bit of a bind here."

"I know, and I'm sorry." Chris felt a pang of guilt at what

he was asking Mason to do, but pressed him anyway. "But it works both ways. I've helped you out in the past. And in the end, it's about getting the job done, right?"

Mason paused. "Let me take a look at what we've got and I'll get back to you. I'll fax you a copy of whatever I find."

"You know what? I can make it easier for you. I'm going to be in your area in about an hour. How about I meet you at your office?"

"Wow, you must really want this information bad. Sure, I'll be here."

"Thanks. And Mason, I owe you one." Chris hung up his cell phone and pulled his truck back on to the highway. *I can't get rid of you, Ray; but you sure as hell won't get rid of me either.*

Chris reflected on what Stephanie and Deanna had both said to him at various times about his preoccupation with work. Could they be right? He was well aware of the risks of burnout in the field of social work. In recent months, he'd found himself increasingly considering a change of career. The problem was, he didn't know what else he wanted to do. He liked his work and over time he'd become good at what he did.

He tried to visualize various possibilities for his future, but his thoughts kept returning to Stephanie. He yearned to spend time with her, to introduce her to Ann Marie, to start a new chapter of his life with her. To his astonishment, he realized that his feelings for Stephanie had manifested themselves in an emotion he had thought he would never experience again— love. His pleasant reverie was jarred by the thought of Ray

Owens. He had to finish his present business with Ray before contemplating any future.

After what seemed like an eternity, Chris reached the corrections building. It felt good to stretch his legs as he walked to the probation office. The receptionist paged Mason, who emerged clutching a thick file. He motioned with his head for Chris to follow him outside where they could talk in private.

"No one's going to know this information came from me, right, Chris?"

Chris reached for the file. "I promise. No one is going to know you and I even talked about Ray Owens. In fact, this conversation never happened." He grinned as they shook hands and parted. He still felt guilty about what he had done. *The end justifies the means,* he told himself, but knew that was a lie.

Back in his truck, he looked through the information Mason had given him. He wasn't surprised to see that the file contained extensive notes on Ray's criminal activities. He ignored the pre-sentence reports from previous criminal convictions and the other court documents; he was interested in only one report. After sifting through the large file, he finally hit paydirt: the report from the Ministry of Child and Family Development. His heart racing, he read page after page in morbid fascination.

Among them was a social worker's report detailing the significant physical and emotional abuse perpetrated against Ray by his foster family, which culminated in his being removed from the home. Chris skimmed through another document, in which a child psychologist who had conducted a battery of tests with Ray concluded that while he was intellectually bright, his fantasies involved aggressive themes. He expressed concern that Ray appeared to be numb to abuse and without normal human emotions.

Chris perused reports outlining Ray's escalating juvenile delinquent history, including property damage at his school and acts of violence against a subsequent foster mother's boyfriend and his foster sister. *Jesus, this is before he even hit sixteen!*

He skipped over Ray's lengthy adult criminal record and related court files until he found a Social History report on Ray's developmental and family history. He hadn't finished reading the first page before his worst fears were realized. Disgusted, he threw the report against his passenger door. *Oh my God, it really is true: Ray is my half-brother.* Would this nightmare ever end? He wished he'd never heard the name Ray Owens. He wished Ray had never been born. He fantasized about a world without Ray.

His cell phone rang, bringing him back to reality. It was Stephanie. What was he going to say to her and how was he going to say it? But she deserved the truth, and taking a deep breath, he answered the phone.

"Where have you been, Chris? I've been trying to reach you forever."

"I'm sorry. I should have called you earlier."

"Oh my God, I couldn't believe when I heard the news. You could have been killed or—"

"I know, Stephanie, I know. Things have been pretty... crazy."

"Are you okay? You sound distracted."

He sighed. "It's a long story."

"You were right all along about that girl, Elizabeth. You

saved her life. That's amazing. Have you read today's paper?"

"No. Should I?"

"Elizabeth gave an interview to the *Sun*. She talked about her time in the cabin and she thanked you again and again. It's a pretty heartbreaking story."

"She went through a lot. More than anyone should ever have to endure." He knew he'd never be able to forget the look of horror on Elizabeth's face when he first saw her at the cabin.

Stephanie paused. "At least they've arrested the people responsible. And Ray has finally left IFP. You get your life back. It's over, Chris. We—"

Chris didn't know if he had the heart or the strength to tell her, but he knew he had to try. "It's not over, Stephanie." He felt defeated as he continued. "This is just the beginning."

"Wha... what do you mean?"

He took a deep breath and told Stephanie about his visit with his father and about his biological relationship with Ray.

Stephanie remained silent for several moments before she said quietly, "Where are you now?"

"I'm sitting in my truck in a probation office parking lot. Staring at a load of papers on Ray."

"Why are you there? You're not working with Ray. He's left IFP, for Christ's sake. You have to leave well enough alone. For your own peace of mind."

Chris braced for the unavoidable clash. "I have to do this. I have no choice. I'd love nothing more than to put an end to all of this and walk away. But Ray won't walk away. He's going to come after me—and everyone close to me. That includes Ann Marie." He paused. "And you, Stephanie. You mean the world to me. I could never live with myself if anything ever happened to you. I have to be ready for him. I *will* be ready for him. And I'll beat that bastard at his own game."

"But what will that make you? That's a slippery slope, Chris. Don't you see that you're obsessed with him?"

"I'm not obsessed, Stephanie. I know him. I *know* what he's trying to do. And I won't let him do it."

"I... I don't know what to say, Chris. I want to be with you, I really do. But listening to you now... makes me realize this isn't possible."

"It is possible. We can make it work. We *can*."

"You're changing, Chris, and it scares me to think just how far you will go with this morbid preoccupation with Ray. He can't do anything now. When he goes to court, he's certain to be found guilty and he'll be going to prison for a long, long time."

"Come on, Stephanie, prison means nothing to him, and neither does time. He'll wait for the right time to move and then he'll act. I *know* it."

He could hear Stephanie weeping. The woman he loved was crying on the other end of the line, and there was nothing he could do to make it better. *Look at what I've done now.* He squeezed his cell phone in anger at himself. *I'm chasing away the woman I love.*

"Stephanie, I'm sorry. I—"

"I'm scared, Chris."

"I'm scared too. I'm terrified of him taking you away from me. I don't want to lose you."

"But Chris, your obsession with Ray *is* taking me away from you. Can't you *see* that?"

"I *can* see that, and I've been racking my brain trying to find a way out of this. And I will find a way, I promise you. I just need you to have faith in me. And I just need some time to come up with the answer." He punched the steering wheel in frustration.

It was Stephanie who finally broke the silence. "My contract with IFP is up in a few weeks. I was offered an extension and was debating whether to accept the offer or return to Corrections Canada." She began to cry. "You're the reason I took the contract at IFP in the first place. And I wanted to discuss this with you tonight, over dinner. I... I foolishly thought we could start a life together." She paused for a moment. "Now I know that's not going to happen."

"Stephanie, please let—"

"Chris, you're spiraling out of control, and there's nothing more I can do to help." She took a deep breath. "I can't bear to stand by helplessly watching you. It would kill me. I... I'm returning to Corrections."

"Stephanie, let's go to dinner tonight. I—"

"No. I don't think that's a good idea. I'm sorry."

"Can I call you later?"

"I don't know. I... I need time to think. I have to go." She hung up.

Alone in his truck in a parking lot full of empty vehicles, Chris felt lost in a world that had become alien to him—a world where his enemy was his brother, and the woman he loved had just walked out on him. He battled to regain perspective in his life, to make sense of what was happening to him.

He lost track of how long he'd been sitting in his truck, which now felt like a prison. The sky had turned from light to dark. People had returned to their cars and left the parking lot. *They* were all moving on with their lives while *he* had nothing to return to. Cell phone still in hand and facing an unknown future, Chris felt like the loneliest person in the world.

His thoughts involuntarily turned to Ray. He wondered what Ray was plotting, alone in his prison cell. And he wondered when their futures would next collide. *I will survive this,* he thought as he drifted off to sleep.


Chris awoke, startled to find himself in his truck. A glance at his watch revealed that it was close to midnight. Wiping the sleep from his eyes, he pulled out of the parking lot and headed back to his apartment. It had been raining steadily while he slept, and he encountered very little traffic on the highway.

Turning on his radio in an attempt to keep awake, he caught highlights of an earlier press conference where an RCMP spokesman provided an update on the investigation into the death of James Carrier and the abduction of his daughter. The newscast left Chris even more depressed as he reflected on the shambles that had become his life. He wondered how it was all going to end, but wasn't particularly optimistic. He was relieved to finally turn onto his street.

Chris yawned as he pulled into the driveway of his building and pressed the opener to the underground parking garage. A drink or two, then to bed, he decided, hoping that things might look better in the morning.

Suddenly his back window exploded, spraying shards of glass everywhere. He glanced in the rear-view mirror just in time to see a shooter taking aim from inside a parked car across the street. Chris ducked as a second bullet ripped through his truck, shattering what remained of the window and coming close enough to spray him with its fragments. *Shit, what do I do now?* He was an open target as long as he remained in his truck. His first impulse was to drive into the parking garage for refuge. But in his panic, he had taken his foot off the brake, sending the truck rolling forward until it had smashed into the side of his building and stalled. The garage was a mere five feet away and the door had opened. He threw open the driver's side door and vaulted from a crouch into the garage.

Once inside, he raced to the main door leading from the garage to the apartment lobby. Too panic-stricken to wait for the elevator, he headed for the stairs. As the stairwell door closed behind him, he thought he heard shouting and more gunfire in the distance. He thundered up flights of stairs, stopping only when he had reached the top. With nowhere else to turn and completely exhausted, he collapsed to the ground and tried to catch his breath.

It was only then that he noticed that he was dripping blood onto the floor and was becoming increasingly weak. He heard strange voices drawing near, but his vision was blurring and he felt woozy. He tried to call out.

And then he felt nothing as his world faded to black.

# FORTY-FIVE

*Thursday, February 23, 7:59 a.m.*

Chris slowly regained consciousness to find himself lying in a hospital bed. Sergeant Ryan was sitting in a chair at the foot of the bed reading a paper—seeing him gave Chris a distinct feeling of déjà vu. When he saw that Chris was awake, the sergeant smiled.

"Good to have you back with us, buddy." He dragged his chair to the side of the bed, then handed the day's *Sun* to Chris. "You've made the headlines... again." The front page displayed a picture of Chris' bullet-ridden truck and went on to report the attack on him the night before.

Chris realized he was once again at the Health Sciences Centre. "What happened, how'd I get here?"

"Glass splinters punctured your skin, and you lost some blood." Brandon looked at Chris' bandaged neck and arms and grinned. "Could have been far worse, of course. They could have scratched your pretty face."

"Come on, Brandon, I'm not in the mood for joking. You

know what I meant. Who did it?"

The sergeant got serious. "The running theory is that Charles Longville tried to eliminate you from his witness list and failed. Fortunately, it's only a matter of time before he's taken into custody himself. The CFSEU suspected Longville might make an attempt on your life, so they stationed officers outside your apartment building as a precaution. The boys moved in and arrested the shooter once he opened fire on you."

Chris was confused. "Hold on. They *knew* someone was being sent to kill me?" He sat up as Brandon's words sunk in. "But they sat back and watched him take potshots at me before they did anything about it? What the hell is that?" His face went red with fury.

Brandon took a moment before responding. "I can't speak for the CFSEU or their actions. What I *can* tell you, though, is that this situation with Longville is highly political, hugely complicated, and you're stuck right in the middle of it all."

"Great! What else is new? Why don't you guys just paint a target on me and be done with it?"

"Chris, if I'd had anything to do with it, I would've done things differently. But the CFSEU is running the investigation now, and I'm not involved. You also have to realize that there's intense pressure to build an ironclad case against Longville. You can be sure he'll bring in a team of lawyers who'll exploit any loophole that helps them shoot down allegations made against him."

He let Chris process that information before continuing. "My guess is that the officers stationed outside your apartment waited until the last possible moment to be absolutely certain you were being targeted, and then they moved in as soon as they could. On the positive side, now they can file additional charges of attempted murder against Longville's associates."

"I'm *so* glad I was able to help." Chris' voice dripped with sarcasm. "Wait a minute. You're not involved in this case at all?"

The sergeant shook his head. "I had to go through a major hassle just to come visit you here today."

"Why?"

"CFSEU Superintendent Patterson is still mad at me for not bringing him into the loop earlier on this case so he denied me access. I went to my superintendent, and from the sound of it, they got into a giant pissing match."

"Who won?"

The sergeant grinned. "Well, I'm here, aren't I?" Then he sighed. "But not in any official capacity. This is their baby. I'm here today... as a friend."

Chris looked at the sergeant with a mixture of surprise and gratitude. "Thanks, Brandon. Really. I could use a friend these days." He paused for a moment. "So what's happening with Ray? Do you know?"

Brandon filled Chris in on the incident at the Pre-Trial Centre.

"Do they think Longville is behind that too?"

"What we know is that the victim was heard to be boasting about the huge payoff he would receive for taking Owens out. We believe one of Longville's men put the word out that their boss wanted Owens killed. Now Longville's struck out twice, and I suspect he's only going to get so many kicks at the can before his associates take care of it for him."

"Great, so I have *that* to look forward to."

"Actually, Chris, I think the pressure's going to ease off you, at least in the short term."

"How's that?"

"Longville hasn't gotten the job done, and that's bound to be making people nervous. So if anyone's feeling the pressure, it's Longville and whoever his source is within the RCMP."

"There's no news on who that source might be?"

"No, but believe me, if we do have a rotten apple in our organization, I'm going to find him before he spoils the whole damn barrel. In any case, where you're concerned, it's likely seen as too risky to warrant anyone taking another shot at you for the foreseeable future. And Owens isn't going anywhere anytime soon, so that takes care of him."

They both sat in silence for a moment. Then Brandon said, "Oh, and here's something you might find amusing. Owens had a weapon—a toothbrush that we believe he smuggled in from IFP. I won't tell you where we think he hid it but it's safe to say both IFP and Corrections are blaming each other for the security breach. Covering their *ass*, if you know what I mean."

"Yeah. Very funny." Chris tried to smile at the news, but failed.

Brandon stared at him. "Is there something you're not telling me?"

Chris shook his head, then filled the sergeant in on what he had discovered about his family connection with Ray. He felt embarrassed acknowledging that the man he hated more than anyone in this world was related to him by blood.

"Wow. I'm really sorry, Chris. That's a pretty big burden to bear." He paused, then pointed to what appeared to be an old mark above his eye. "We all have our scars. Some are just more visible than others. You'll get through this. You're a survivor."

Chris wanted to ask about his friend's scar, but now was not the right time. He pondered Brandon's statement about being a survivor. With his seemingly endless stream of problems, Chris had been feeling more like a victim. But it occurred to him now that Brandon was right, that he had successfully come through each encounter and the experience had made him stronger.

The two friends sat there silently for a few minutes, both contemplating the implications of being targeted by a psychopath. Finally, Brandon placed his hand on Chris' shoulder. "Whatever happens, you won't be alone."

"Thanks, Brandon. I appreciate it."

"Don't mention it, buddy. The fact of the matter is, I think we make a great team."

Chris reflected for a minute. "You know what? I feel the same way."

The sergeant grinned. "And don't forget, you owe me a beer." He looked down at the newspaper. "That reminds me: a reporter's been waiting outside hoping to land an interview with you. What do you want to do?"

Chris gave a weary sigh. "I'm not interested in talking to anybody. Can you—"

"Send him away? Sure. It'll be my pleasure. We'll talk soon." With a parting wave, Brandon left the room.

Chris lay back in his bed and shut his eyes, hoping to get some rest. He heard a light knock and the door slowly opening. Thinking it was the reporter, he was preparing to launch into a protest when, to his pleasant surprise, he saw it was Deanna and Ann Marie in the doorway.

His eyes met his daughter's. She looked scared. "Hey, sweetie, come on in. It's okay." Deanna was visibly upset, so he attempted a joke: "I just can't get enough of this place. How did you know I was here?"

"The hospital called early this morning." She looked pointedly at the newspaper on Chris' bed. "Besides, it's hard to miss when you're on the front page."

"Well, I'm glad you came." He could see that Ann Marie was apprehensive about coming closer to him. Figuring that his bandages were making her uncomfortable, he said gently, "It's okay, Ann. I had a bit of an accident, but everything's all right now."

"Did a bad guy try to hurt you, Daddy?"

Chris wasn't sure how to respond. He finally opted for a sanitized version of the truth to try to reassure her. "Yes, sweetie. But the police caught him, and he's not going to hurt anyone anymore."

"Does it hurt?" She pointed to his neck.

"No. They've taken really good care of me, and hopefully I'll get to go home soon."

Deanna looked at Chris. "The doctor said you're free to go anytime now. We'll give you a ride home."

Ann Marie looked excitedly at her mother. "Can Daddy come home with us?"

Chris rescued Deanna from the awkward situation. "Sweetie, I need to go to my own home today. But I'll see you on Saturday, right?"

"Okay." She looked disappointed, but then perked up. "Can we go to Wilbur's on Saturday?"

He laughed. "We sure can. They should give us our own

table after all the times we've been there, don't you think?"

The smile returned to Ann Marie's face. "I like going there with you, Daddy."

"Yeah, me too." Chris smiled back. "So, how about we get out of here?"

Charles Longville hurried about his mansion. He had some serious damage control to deal with. When he'd learned from his source at the RCMP that Ray's cell phone had been recovered, he knew it would only be a matter of time before the police connected it to him unless he acted swiftly and diverted the investigation.

He wasn't sure who he detested more—Ray Owens or Chris Ryder. He'd ordered them both killed, but the bastards had an uncanny knack for survival. Well, they weren't the only ones with nine lives. Longville was working feverishly on his contingency plan. With Pierce Hennessy in police custody, Longville would work to pin the whole affair on Hennessy and his goons. He knew he had to make the phone disappear once and for all to completely evade prosecution, but his snitch at the RCMP had not returned his calls all day. *Who the hell does he think he is!* Longville knew there was only one thing he could do—pay his pet cop a personal visit and remind him where his money was coming from.

He grabbed the keys to his BMW and opened the front door, only to be greeted by a man he recognized as one of Hennessy's associates. "What the hell are you doing here?" Longville was livid. "I thought I made myself clear to your boss that no one *ever* makes direct contact with me. And what do you do? You show up at my bloody *house*. Get in here." The two men entered, and Longville slammed the door behind them. "Why aren't you going after Chris Ryder? Your boss is going to hear about this, believe me." Only after the door was closed did he realize that his visitor had not come empty-handed.

"My boss sent me to deliver a message. Ryder's not a problem right now. *You* are."

Longville struggled to come to terms with what was happening. There had to be a way for him to walk away from this situation. But for once he came up empty—no solution, no contingency plan, nothing. And in the split second before the bullet shattered his skull, Longville realized that, for the first and last time in his life, he was powerless.

At home, Chris was intent on doing little more than resting his exhausted body. He retrieved a message from Gerald wishing him a speedy recovery and was about to lie down when the phone rang.

The caller identified himself as a guard at the Pre-Trial Correctional Centre. "Are you Chris Ryder?"

"Yeah. Why?" Chris' heart hammered in his chest. *What the hell has Ray done now?*

"We have a Ray Owens here who wants to talk with his brother. We've been instructed to supervise his calls, and you're on his no-contact list unless you want to hear from him. Are you his brother?"

*This has to be some kind of sick joke.* Reluctantly he forced out the words. "Yeah, I'm his brother."

"Will you accept a call from him?"

Chris hesitated. He didn't want to accept *anything* from Ray and he wasn't in the mood for any more of Ray's twisted games. At the same time, he was curious as to why he was calling.

"Mr. Ryder, are you still there?"

"I'm still here."

"Will you accept a call from Ray Owens?"

"Yeah, put him through."

There was a clicking sound, followed by a brief silence and then, "Ryder? How's my famous brother?"

"What do you want, Ray?"

Ray snickered. "I heard about the excitement at your apartment building and naturally I had to make sure you were okay."

"Get to your point or I'm hanging up."

More laughter. "I had some excitement too. Seems the late great Charles Longville was not very happy with the likes of me. But as the saying goes, you can't keep a good man down. And I hear Longville got what was coming to him."

"What are you talking about?"

"Oh, I guess you haven't heard, what with being in hospital and all. Our man, Charles in Charge, took one for the team. Which means, dear brother, that you have moved up a notch in my to-do list, and I will admit you're becoming a worthy adversary."

Chris felt a raging headache coming on and walked to his bathroom in search of an ibuprofen. Grabbing the television remote, he flipped through channels until he found a local station highlighting breaking news about the murder of Charles Longville. Stunned, he thought back to the conversation he'd had with Sergeant Ryan earlier that day. It looked like Longville's criminal activities had finally caught up with him, and his RCMP snitch had him killed because his ties to organized crime made him too much of a risk to his associates. Chris hoped fervently that Longville's death signaled an end to any interest they might have with him.

"Hey, Ryder, you still there? Or am I calling you at a bad time?" Ray's sarcastic voice interrupted Chris' thoughts. Chris looked with surprise at the phone still in his hand; he had forgotten about it. Time to hang up—but not before igniting some fireworks of his own.

"Listen, Ray. I know you're pretty bored, but you'd better get used to your new home because you're going to be spending a whole lot of time there. I have to go, so I'll let you get back to your cell."

There was silence on the other end. For an instant, Chris wondered if he'd hung up. Then Ray responded coldly, "I'll make you a promise, Ryder. I won't be spending much time here. I'm looking forward to my day in court, and I'm absolutely sure I won't be doing any hard time. And when I'm finished in court, you and the fucking IFP will be the laughing stock of the goddamn country."

"And how do you figure that, Ray?"

"Just you wait and see, *asshole!*"

Chris could sense that Ray was on the verge of a meltdown. "Sounds to me like you're getting upset. Anything bothering you? Maybe you need to take an anger management course. I hear they have those in prison."

"*Fuck you,* Ryder. You're the reason I'm in this hole, and I promise you'll pay! Big time!"

"Me? Last time I checked, it was you who pulled the

trigger on James Carrier. Don't try to pull me into your twisted little life. You're the only one responsible."

"You got all the breaks! Everything was given to you on a silver fucking platter while I've had to fight to take what is mine. I—"

"Come on, Ray, we all deal with the hand we're given. My—"

"They chose *you*, Ryder, over *me*. You don't know what that's like... *but you soon will*!" Ray screamed so loudly that Chris thought the guard would terminate the call. "You had a family, while I was shunted around foster homes like a leper, a nobody, *a piece of shit*. And I got the shit kicked out of me everywhere I went—at home, at school. And it *pissed me off!*"

Ray took a deep breath, then added more calmly, "But you know what I did with all that anger? As you mindfuckers like to say, I found an *outlet* for it—I learned to fight and started hitting back. The bullied became the bully, and I've never looked back. Nothing gives me more *fucking* satisfaction than unleashing my rage on others, and seeing their pain. And I'll tell you something else. I learned to rely on no one but myself. I got used to being alone. I embraced it. In fact, you want to know something? I prefer being alone."

He lowered his voice almost to a whisper. "I'll let you in on a little secret, Ryder. I'm going to show you what it's like to be alone. You'll learn to embrace it too. You're going to die a pathetic old man—just like *our* old man. I heard you saw him recently. Hah, I've got plans for him too."

"Why, Ray? What will that prove?" Chris found himself wondering why he wanted to understand Ray and why, in particular, he wanted to help Ray understand the consequences of his actions.

"It'll complete the cycle, Ryder. We're born alone, and we die alone. In the end, nothing matters worth *shit*."

"What matters, Ray, is what we do with the time in between. That is our choice. Your choice. My choice. And we live with the consequences of those choices."

"You don't get it, do you? My choice is to take *away* your choice, brother. I'm going to take away everything you've got. Your family—"

"You leave my family out of this! *You hear me*?"

"Who needs the anger management courses now?" Ray howled with laughter. "But yeah, you brought up a good point. Maybe I should look into taking some courses while I'm here. I wonder whether your fuck-buddy, Stephanie, will be running any courses. I hear she's coming out this way."

The blood rushed from Chris' head. His legs would no longer support him and he collapsed onto his couch. *Oh my God, the bastard's going after Stephanie.* He desperately tried to reassure himself that every precaution would be taken to ensure Stephanie and Ray would never cross paths at Corrections Canada. He'd suspected all along that this was how Ray operated in terrorizing his victims, but it was small comfort now to have pegged him so accurately. *Get control of yourself! Don't let Ray win!* He took a deep breath. "It's good that you're thinking about your future, but it's going to be behind bars. And since you've been so full of promises, I'll make you one. I promise that I'll do everything under the sun to keep you locked up and away from my family." Chris heard the guard in the background giving Ray the two-minute warning to wrap up his conversation.

Then Ray was back on the line. "We'll soon see. I'll be out, and before you know it, we'll be catching up on old times.

Who knows? Maybe you can introduce me to your daughter. It's Ann Marie, isn't it?"

Chris placed the phone an arm's length away and took several deep breaths to keep from losing control. He knew he had to change his tactics with Ray, to not react to his threats. "That's right. Keep on talking. The difference is, I have a life and you're gonna *get* life." Ray's cursing cheered him immensely. Chris felt as if he'd been sparring with a master and had finally uncovered his strategy and gained the upper hand. "You can play all the games you want. But we both know I'm right. You're going to jail for a long time. You'd better get used to it."

"This isn't over, Ryder. *It isn't fucking over!*" Ray screamed.

Chris said calmly, "Actually, Ray, it is today."

And then he hung up.

Long after he'd hung up the phone, Chris continued thinking about Ray. He wasn't surprised that Ray refused to accept any responsibility for his actions, but it concerned him that Ray personally blamed him—Chris—for all his problems. And Chris knew two things for sure: Ray's way of seeking revenge involved going after his family; and Ray would never give up or go down without a fight.

It was fate that brought Ray crashing into his world. And for the foreseeable future, their fates would be intertwined. But so what? He'd survived everything that had been thrown his way over the last two weeks and had emerged with a newfound inner strength and an emerging sense of hope that when he next crossed paths with Ray, he'd be ready.

Chris still had the phone in his hand when it rang again. Suspecting it was Ray calling back, he resisted the impulse to fling the phone across the room. Instead, he calmly pressed the talk button and waited for his caller to identify himself.

"Chris? Is everything okay?" came Stephanie's voice.

Chris was relieved it was not Ray, and surprised to hear from Stephanie. It took him a few seconds to refocus his thoughts. "Sorry about that, Stephanie. How are you?" He exhaled deeply and his heart rate slowly returned to normal.

"Never mind me. How are *you* doing? I called the hospital, but they said you'd already been discharged."

"Oh, you know, a little shaken up, but I'll be all right. It's going to be okay. It really is."

"You sound... different."

Chris knew Stephanie could read him better than anyone. "I *feel* different, Stephanie. But in a good way." Chris didn't know how to elaborate any further at that moment, so he didn't.

Stephanie broke the silence. "Chris, I'd like to see you."

He detected a peculiar tone in her voice. "I'd like to see you, too. Do you want to get together for coffee tomorrow?" Her silence startled him. "Stephanie, are—"

"I need to see you today, Chris."

"Okay. Today would be great. Where are you? I can—"

"I'm outside your building. Can you buzz me in?"

The wait for Stephanie's elevator to reach his floor was the longest two minutes of Chris' life. As he stood in the open doorway of his apartment, his mind raced through a million possible reasons for her visit. Finally Stephanie emerged from the elevator and walked down the hallway toward him. His heart sank at the look of uncertainty clouding her face.

Before he had a chance to say anything, Stephanie said, "Chris, I came here against my better judgment. I really don't know if this is the right thing for me to do." She stood with one foot planted inside Chris' apartment door, the other in the hallway. "I *love* you. And right now, I feel that I want to be with you always." Tears glistened in her eyes. "But I'm afraid of how I'm going to feel about this tomorrow."

Chris whispered softly into her ear, "I love you, too, Stephanie. We can deal with tomorrow, tomorrow." He wrapped his arms around her and led her into his apartment.

## ACKNOWLEDGEMENTS

This book would not have been written without the enduring support of so many amazing people.

Thanks to Barbara Carew, Alan Carew, Tanya Carew, Lauren Carew, Matthew Carew, Andrew Pike, Nicole Reid, T.Rae Mitchell, Tony Mitchell (Original Mix Design), Dion Tilley (Standard Rich and Famous), Cheryl Freedman, Elaine Freedman, Robin Spano, Garry Ryan, Debra Purdy Kong, Raquel Larsen, John Thistle, Donna Proctor, Rob Proctor, Leanne Wilson, Don Kerr, Paul Matwychuk, Matt Bowes, Greg Vickers, Gary Wilson, and the staff at NeWest Press, LeeAnne Meldrum, Eugene Wang, Bryna Dominguez, Roger Sasaki, Lynda Jordan, Shirley Skidmore, Crime Writers of Canada, Crime Writers Association, and the Federation of BC Writers. I sincerely apologize to anyone I may have missed this go around. A huge "Thank You" goes out to booksellers and readers!

While this book references real-life institutions and media outlets, the events and characters are fictitious. The author would like to acknowledge the Combined Forces Special Enforcement Unit (CFSEU) and Robert Hare (Psychopathy Checklist, Revised).

**D.B. CAREW** has his masters degree in social work from Dalhousie University and currently works at a forensic psychiatric hospital in Port Coquitlam, B.C. An avid runner, he is a member of the Crime Writers of Canada and the Federation of B.C. Writers. *The Killer Trail* is his first novel.